PRAISE FOR LAKE OF DESTINY

"Delightful, charming, and heartwarming!"

—NEW YORK TIMES BESTSELLING AUTHOR
WENDY HIGGINS

*"I adored every page . . .Beautifully written, perfectly paced
with traces of magical realism.*

—AWARD-WINNING AUTHOR ERIN CASHMAN

*"Well-written, well-crafted, well-paced and full of
heart. . . . So much charm it's magical!"*

—BOOKGEEK

*"Martina Boone's gorgeous storytelling enthralled me from
start to finish. The plot is captivating, whimsical, and full of
surprises that kept me turning the pages."*

—SINCERELY KARENJO REVIEWS

*"I loved this!!! It reminds me of a Nora Roberts series, The
Gallaghers of Ardmore . . . but a Scottish version with men
in kilts!"*

—TWO CHICKS ON BOOKS REVIEWS

PRAISE FOR COMPULSION

"Skillfully blends rich magic and folklore with adventure, sweeping romance, and hidden treasure . . . An impressive start to the Heirs of Watson Island series."

—*PUBLISHER'S WEEKLY*

"Eight Beaufort is so swoon-worthy that it's ridiculous. Move over Four, Eight is here to stay!"

—*RT BOOK REVIEWS*, RT EDITORS BEST BOOKS OF 2014

"Boone's Southern Gothic certainly delivers a compelling mystery about feuding families and buried secrets, not to mention a steamy romance."

—*BOOKLIST*

"Even the villains and not-likable characters were just so engrossing. I have to say I've already put the sequel on my TBR shelf."

—*USA TODAY*

"This Southern gothic mixes dark spirits, romance, feuding families and ancient curses into the perfect potion."

—*JUSTINE MAGAZINE*

"*Darkly romantic and steeped in Southern Gothic charm, you'll be compelled to get lost in the Heirs of Watson Island series.*"

—#1 NEW YORK TIMES BESTSELLING AUTHOR
JENNIFER L. ARMENTROUT

"*The perfect Southern family saga: charming and steamy on the surface, with cold-blooded secrets buried down deep.*"

—KENDARE BLAKE, NYT BESTSELLING AUTHOR OF
THREE DARK CROWNS AND ANNA DRESSED IN BLOOD

"*A fresh twist on the Southern Gothic— haunting, atmospheric, and absorbing.*"

—CLAUDIA GRAY, NYT BESTSELLING AUTHOR OF
A THOUSAND PIECES OF YOU AND
THE EVERNIGHT AND SPELLCASTER SERIES

"*Beautifully written, with vivid characters, a generations-old feud, and romance that leaps off the page, this Southern ghost story left me lingering over every word, and yet wanting to race to the compelling finish. Martina Boone's Compulsion is not to be missed.*"

—MEGAN SHEPHERD, NYT BESTSELLING AUTHOR OF
THE CAGE SERIES AND THE MADMAN'S DAUGHTER

MAGIC OF WINTER

Also By Martina Boone

Lake of Destiny: A Celtic Legends Novel

Bell of Eternity: A Celtic Legends Novel

Compulsion

Persuasion

Illusion

MAGIC OF WINTER

—A CELTIC LEGENDS NOVEL—

MARTINA BOONE

MAYFAIR
PUBLISHING

Magic of Winter is a work of fiction, and the characters, events, and places depicted in it are products of the author's imagination. Where actual events, places, organizations, or persons, living or dead, are included, they are used fictitiously and not intended to be taken otherwise.

MAYFAIR
PUBLISHING
712 H Street NE, Suite 1014,
Washington, DC 20002
First Mayfair Publishing edition April 2017
Copyright © 2017 by Martina Boone

Jacket design by Kalen O'Donnell
Interior Design by Rachel & Joel Greene

Published in the United States of America
ISBN 978-1-946773-06-7 (trade paperback)

For Hailey, for all her much appreciated cheerleading.

MAGIC OF WINTER

HOMECOMING

"Lilting wildly up the glen;
But aye to me he sings a song;
Will ye no come back again?"

CAROLINA OLIPHANT NAIRNE.
AKA MRS. BOGAN OF BOGAN

L IKE THE DUSTING OF SNOWFLAKES falling around her, a sense of homecoming settled over Cait as she turned off the highway and drove into the glen. Fifteen months of exile swept away. The swelling snow-capped braes that rimmed the valley, the blue-ice sheen of the frozen lochs, the smoke curling from the handful of homes and businesses that lay along the one-lane main road passing through Balwhither village; Cait loved every inch so much it hurt. Beneath the holiday lights that were just beginning to shine in the gloaming and the last rays of winter sun that painted the clouds in scarlet, it all looked just as her heart remembered.

It should have been different. She should have been different. The realization that nothing had changed, that she hadn't changed, left her chilled.

As if she sensed Cait's distress, the cat in the carrier beside her gave a plaintive Siamese wail. Because there was no ignoring Mrs. Bogan of Bogan when she wasn't pleased, Cait eased her finger through the grating before the protests could grow any louder.

She stroked the velvet chocolate-colored nose. "Be patient a wee bit longer, love. We'll be there soon enough."

Mrs. Bogan flattened her ears and sent her mistress an arctic, cross-eyed stare of abject misery.

Cait smiled faintly, but she was fairly well sick of being trapped in the car herself. For miles now, she'd craved a hot shower and an early bedtime almost as much as she needed the reassurance of seeing her father face-to-face. After he'd rung to cancel his trip to London the night before, she had barely slept.

She'd been in the mini-kitchen of her cupboard-sized bedsit above an Indian restaurant north of Croydon, doing her best to figure out her mother's holiday shortbread recipe as a surprise for his arrival when she'd picked up the phone. "Are you nearly ready, then?" she'd asked. "What time are you leaving in the morning?"

"I'm sorry," he'd said, his voice quieter than the booming rumble that usually came from his burly chest, "but I've bad news to deliver. Mairi's off sick with flu and Kirsty is due to have her bairn soon. She can't work more hours at the Tea Room, so I won't be coming down."

Cait had gone stiff, not because of the news so much as because of the tension she sensed. "Close up, then. Come down anyway. No one will notice much if you close between now and Hogmanay, and I've made a long list of all the out-of-the-way places I want to show you. Things we can do. I've hunted out some second-hand bookshops, too, where we can pick up new books for the lending library and send you home with your car fully packed."

"I can't, Caitie." Her father hesitated. "The glen is fair full of tourists now, what with one thing or another. I can't afford to miss out on the income."

"Then I'll come home and help," Cait said, her stomach sinking at the thought.

"You don't want to do that. We'd have no real time to see each other."

"I won't let you be alone for Christmas."

"And I won't have you driving all the way up here, spending your hard-earned money, only to be miserable. Consider it. With events in the village nearly every night, you'll not be able to avoid seeing Brice."

Cait's stomach clenched at the sound of her ex-fiancé's name. Even after fifteen months there was both pain and pleasure in it. But she could manage. "I'm over all that," she said. "I can't stay away forever."

"Come next year, then." There was a note of something akin to desperation in her father's voice, and Cait had the same niggling feeling she'd been harboring for a while in their daily conversations, that no matter how much he denied it, there was something not quite right.

"Are you sure there's nothing wrong at home apart from Mairi's flu?" she asked. "What are you trying not to tell me?"

"What could be wrong? Och, you're getting to be as much of a worrier as your mother, God rest her. Now I had better ring off—"

"Fine, but I'll see you two days from now, by dinnertime," Cait had said, "and that's the end of the argument. We can go to the tree lighting in the village together, the two of us."

She'd rung off before he could protest more, and she'd finished baking the cookies and done a round of nervous cleaning all around the flat. But after going to bed, she'd lain awake in the dark and realized she didn't believe a single word he'd said.

With school out for the break, surely there should have been someone who could come in to help at the Library and Tea Room? And outside of the high season in the warm months, business was never brisk. The village had been working to change that, but even so, there would be few enough visitors willing to brave the wilds of the Scottish Highlands at Christmastime. She'd known that at the time her father said it, and looking around now at the quiet glen, she confirmed it.

Whatever was keeping her father in Balwhither had nothing to do with flu or tourists. Cait would wager a bottle of Donald Fletcher's favorite Dalwhinnie single malt on that.

Her hot shower would have to wait a little longer.

"We are going to need to take a detour, you and I," she said to Mrs. Bogan, pushing her antique Mini Copper a little faster. "I'll make it up to you later with extra fish."

Accustomed to being waited on hand and paw, Mrs. Bogan was unimpressed. She averted her narrow face and cursed Cait with a string of expletives that required no translation.

Cait's half-smile didn't last very long. The stretch of road she was traveling was too close to the turnoff toward the parish church and the ancient cemetery.

In the fading light, snow dusted the tops of the gravestones like confectioner's sugar and lay undisturbed along the track, giving silent testimony to the absence of any visitors coming to see the grave of Robert Roy MacGregor, whose already legendary status Liam Neeson had only elevated on the movie screen. But that wasn't the grave that was on Cait's mind.

Her mum and her own Robbie both lay buried in the newer cemetery behind the modern church, her brother dead these past three years. When Cait had last set foot in Balwhither, the heather had been in full bloom on the braes and her mother had been newly laid to rest. Cait had left the burial with her heart broken only to have it broken again by Brice MacLaren the very next afternoon.

She let out a shaky breath. How was it possible to still feel so much after all this time? Pain and joy and grief and rage so thick they all blurred together? Shouldn't she have a better grasp on healing?

Shaking her head, she sent another sidelong glance at Mrs. Bogan. "You see? This is why I've stayed away. Maybe Dad wasn't wrong in thinking I wasn't ready."

Well, she'd have to make the best of it. Come New Year's Day, she and Mrs. Bogan would drive south again, back to London where no one would dissect her every misstep and mistake and speculate about why she'd left Brice a month before the wedding. And if, a small voice in Cait's head protested, such freedom came at the price of a cramped bedsit with broken heating and sky-high rent and no one she trusted enough to so much as feed her cat, that was fine. Brilliant. In London, she didn't run the risk of having to face Brice himself. Her father was right. At this time of year, there'd be no way to avoid the man.

"Still, I am an adult," she told the cat. "How hard can this be? I will be perfectly polite. I'll smile and keep my composure. And I won't waste a second feeling sorry for myself. Not one wee bit."

She drove on, and at the intersection of the only two roads in the village, she kept her foot on the brake barely long enough to scan the cars parked in front of the Last Stand Inn and Tavern, the whitewashed inn that had been expanding room by room since before the first of the Jacobite Risings. Brice's old Toyota truck was nowhere in sight, so either he was still working at the garage, or he'd driven down to the pub with someone else. With luck, that meant Cait could dart into the Tea Room, find her father, and get back home for the hot shower she'd been craving without seeing so much as a whisker of the cheating snake.

Facing him in person wasn't the only obstacle,

though. The memories were impossible to escape now that she was here. The high rock wall at the back of the Inn's courtyard was where Brice had kissed her for the first time when she was ten. A few yards farther, an empty stretch of snow-covered grass led down to the side of Loch Fàil, the long thin lake that ran through most of the glen until it met the smaller, plumper Loch Daoine. Between the two, a narrow peninsula held the stone where the legend of the Beltane "Sighting" had been inscribed so many centuries ago that no one remembered who had etched it there. Cait was one of the few girls in the glen who had never lined up on the banks of the loch on Beltane morning, hoping to glimpse the face of the man she was meant to love. Not because she didn't believe, but because she didn't need help from beyond to tell her what she'd been certain she knew already.

Jaw set, she turned into the carpark for the Library and Tea Room across the road and pulled to a stop in front of the building that had been so much a part of her life, her mother's life. Of their life together. It seemed impossible to think her mum wasn't still there, waiting to dispense, as if by magic, the perfect book to anyone who drifted through the door for a cuppa and a scone or a bit of cake. And Cait couldn't helping remembering a moment, not long after her mother had fallen ill, one of those rare times when the Tea Room was empty of both villagers and tourists. Like now, the snow and the sun had both been coming down, and her mum had stood with a pencil behind her ear and her favorite blue apron tied over her slacks, steam from the cup cradled between her hands rising in curls to fog the pane of glass.

"We could close early," Cait had said, coming to stand beside her. "The snow will keep everyone away."

"Don't ever forget to appreciate this—all of it." Her mum had gestured across at the view of the glittering lochs, and she'd set down the cup and turned to Cait. "Winter's a gift in the Highlands. The big cities change, the whole world changes, in the wink of an eye. But here in the glen, the winters are a reminder that, as bleak and dark as life can seem, we'll get through it. There's beauty in the worst of things."

That could have summed up Morag Fletcher's entire life. She'd always looked for the best in every situation, in every person, and her curiosity was insatiable. She'd dreamed of traveling, of seeing all the places she'd read about in the books she loved, but Cait's father had never had any interest in leaving the glen. When his own father died and they inherited the old Fletcher house together, instead of living here and keeping the views to herself, Morag had talked him into converting the house into a tea room and private lending library full of cozy rooms where all the people of the glen could read about the places she herself would never visit.

The structure hadn't changed much since Cait had seen it last. Apart from the wooden trim that her mum had painted shocking pink to attract the tourists, it still looked like a grand old home with pale gray stone walls, mullioned windows, and a high gabled roof. That pink color was peeling and a little faded, but the LIBRARY AND TEA ROOM sign above the door still looked fresh in the gold and silver paint that had been one of the last projects Cait and her mum had done together.

There should have been cars in the lot at this time of day, and customers. Not a single light shone in any of the rooms, though, and through the windows in the main dining area, Cait could see that someone had stacked the tables and chairs in the middle of the room. Clearly, the place hadn't been used in quite some time.

A painful knot settled in her midsection.

She had known, deep down, that the Tea Room wouldn't—couldn't—be the same without her mum. Her father didn't have the same gift for books, nor the same passion or anything approaching Morag's knowledge. But he'd always worked harder than anyone Cait had ever known, and on the rare occasions when he chose to keep his opinions to himself, he could charm the knickers off an elephant. The idea that, after all his protests of keeping it open, the place would be closed when it should have been full of people had never occurred to Cait.

Easing herself out of the car, she tried to keep from panicking. A bitter wind off the lochs raised goosebumps on her flesh, and she fought to suck in a lungful of air so cold it burned.

That was good, though. She needed to clear her head before she went and faced him. Turning her back on the empty building, she strode across the street.

Hadn't she known for months something was wrong?

Why had she let herself believe his assurances?

Her father had always been as stubborn as that old orange bull of Davy Grigg's that Brice and his cousin Brando had tried to tip in the pasture one night when they were ten. And though she'd wanted to hope that things had improved between them since she'd walked away from Brice, maybe she'd only been fooling herself.

In a way, that night of bull-tipping had been the root of all the problems. Amid the disaster that prank of Brice's had set in motion, a nine-year-old Cait, half bookworm and half wild, untamable tomboy, had fallen head-over-heels in love with him and never fallen out again. She'd loved the way he didn't back down even when everybody blamed him, the way he'd tried to protect his cousin Brando. The courage and defiance of him. But everything she admired in him all those years, her father had seen as unsteadiness. A lack of moral fiber. The way she'd championed Brice, defended him, had driven a wedge between her dad and herself.

And, of course, Brice had eventually proven her father right. What she'd taken for courage had turned out to be nothing more than selfishness and lack of responsibility.

She refused—refused—to put any more distance in their relationship because of Brice MacLaren.

If her father was afraid she would fall right back into Brice's arms, he couldn't be more mistaken.

How dare he lie to her?

What he'd told her wasn't a simple fib. He'd told her an out-and-out porker about needing to keep the Library and Tea Room open, and to cover up for that, he'd done his best to convince her not to bother coming home.

The man had explaining to do.

And the explanation had better be a good one.

BLINDNESS

*"Had we never lov'd sae blindly,
Never met—or never parted—
we had ne'er been broken-hearted."*

ROBERT BURNS

B RICE MACLAREN HAD SPENT MONTHS
refurbishing an original 1980 Marv IV Mini for
Cait the year she'd finished at university. After
finding the car in a junk lot in Liverpool, he'd towed
it back to Balwhither, rebuilt the engine, scavenged
interior parts from eleven different cars, and banged
out and painted the exterior himself in racing green
with stripes. Every nook and cranny of the Mini was
familiar to him, and there was no mistaking it when he
spotted the car parked in front of the Library and Tea
Room.

She wasn't due home for another day, though,

according to her father.

Gripping the wheel of his Land Rover Discovery, Brice cursed himself and scanned the windows of the building as he drove toward it, looking for a telltale light inside.

He hated to think how Cait would feel if she saw the mess and the FOR SALE sign in the window before anyone had explained the situation. He'd meant to get out here first thing this morning to keep that very thing from happening, but his client had stopped by the garage wanting to check progress on the 1964 Aston Martin DB5 that Brice had promised to finish for Christmas delivery. The visit should have taken an hour at most, but he'd had to spend so long going over every fine point of the restoration work that it had eaten most of the day. Then the man had pulled out a bottle of twenty-four-year-old Bruichladdich single malt along with an order for an even more expensive car, and that had taken still more time. Brice'd had to ring Donald to promise he'd work through the night to get the Tea Room looking a bit more like it was open for business, if that was what it took, and he had intended to keep that promise.

Not that he agreed with Donald trying to lie to Cait. He didn't. If he'd had any idea that Donald hadn't told Cait he meant to sell the business, that the daft man hadn't told Cait anything, Brice would never have agreed to help with the renovation in the first place. Which, of course, the old goat had known well enough when he'd bullied Brice into pulling out all the old bookshelves and everything that had given the place its character. Everything Cait's mother had done.

Cait would murder both Brice and her father in slow and painful inches when she found out.

Thinking of seeing her, the old anger and emptiness suddenly flooded back after long months where there'd been only determination. Cait had been a part of him for so long, he still didn't know how to be without her.

And thinking of her, it was as if he'd managed to conjure her out of mist. Something moved on the loch side of the road opposite the Tea Room, a figure with glossy dark hair, dark trousers, and a black jumper that blended into the descending night. Cait's achingly familiar face gleaming pale.

He swerved to avoid her, and the Land Rover sent up a sheet of slush that sprayed her from waist to feet.

She whipped around as if she would attack the car, long hair flying in a curtain, blue eyes wild as fire, and a screech loud enough to carry over the engine's growl. And just like that, the same as the sight of her had done every day since he was ten years old, Brice found it impossible to process a coherent thought.

Aye, God, but he had missed her.

At the same time, he wished she hadn't come. Not yet.

A muscle twitching in his cheek, he pulled the Land Rover to a stop alongside her Mini and jumped out onto the tarmac. It was only then that he caught his first real look at her. Cait. She was stooped over, wiping at the slush to dry herself off as much as she could manage.

He took off his coat and hurried toward her.

The pull between them hadn't changed a whit. The closer he approached, the more his body remembered what he'd spent fifteen months trying to forget: the curve of cheeks that fit perfectly against his palms, full lips that offered arguments and kisses with equal passion, a stubborn chin she used to fake a confidence she often didn't have.

She straightened as he reached the road. Glared at him. "Do you never grow up, Brice MacLaren? I suppose this is your childish way of getting even?"

Well, that was calmer than he'd expected.

"Christ, Cait—I'm sorry. Here, take this." He draped his coat across her shoulders, careful not to touch her. "I didn't see you standing there."

"You might have if you weren't driving your usual ridiculous speed." Cait's hands went up as if to snatch the coat away. She was shivering, though, her teeth chattering, and she seemed to realize that suddenly. Instead of throwing the coat at him as he'd half-expected, she drew it closer around herself and burrowed down into it the way she'd burrowed into his coats a hundred times before.

The loss of her hit him all over again. "I was going the limit," he said, sounding tired even to himself, "and I thought you weren't coming until tomorrow."

"How'd you know I was coming at all?" She went still, her attention sharpening.

"The glen's still small. That hasn't changed. But it's good you're home—your father's missed you. I've missed you."

"You lost the right to miss me when you threw what we had away. If you ever felt anything for me at all. And if you're thinking I've been neglecting my father, you couldn't be more wrong."

He'd forgotten that eyes could burn so bright and still be cold. "I never said you were neglecting him."

"You implied it."

"Don't go putting words in my mouth, woman. If you're hearing them, that's your own conscience talking and nothing to do with me." Brice raised his hands and shook his head. "No, look, let's not do this. I didn't even mean to say that."

"Och, but you've always been brilliant at saying things, doing things, you don't mean and can't take back." Cait's face tipped up to his, snowflakes melting on her cheeks. Then her expression twisted, and she stared down at the tips of her high-heeled boots and the sodden hem of her expensive trousers, clothes more fashionable than the jeans she'd always worn before she went to London. "You're right, though," she said, "I promised myself I wouldn't argue with you, and I can't seem to help it. We should just keep out of each other's way while I'm here."

"No, it's past time we talked. Preferably somewhere your teeth can stop chattering instead of out here in the street screeching at each other, though."

"I do not screech. I never screech." Her eyes flashed again, fire and ice and temper.

He raised an eyebrow at her, grinning. Waiting for her to laugh.

There was a time she would have. A time when they would have laughed together. Now her triangular face pinched even tighter and her chest heaved as though she'd run the circumference of the glen.

He wanted to tuck her against his chest and hold her. Wanted to never let her go.

Instead, he stood like a pillock with the words trapped in his brain and refusing to come out. In the months since she'd gone to London, he'd bottled up too many things he had to tell her. Too many questions.

Was she sorry she had left him? Did she regret jumping to conclusions, the half-coherent accusations she'd slipped into his mailbox? Didn't she realize her father had taken advantage of her weakness and her doubt?

Donald Fletcher had been only too happy to tell Brice what he'd said to Cait the day after her mother's funeral when she'd come storming home. It hadn't been much worse than the things he'd already told them both a hundred times before, but with her mother freshly buried, Cait had been out of her head with grief and vulnerable.

It had taken months for Brice to understand that. All he'd known at first was that Cait's leaving had ripped open an empty space inside him. And without her there, he'd had nothing to fill that emptiness. Nothing worthwhile. Which had only proven that Cait's father had been right all along in saying that Brice didn't have anything real to offer her.

He was working on that, though. Determined to change it. Determined to change himself.

Standing on the snowy tarmac, nearly toe to toe with her, he tried to find a way to say so.

She tapped her foot against the pavement, her shoulders thrown back. Her fighting stance. Her invitation to a brawl.

The loch gleamed dark behind her, reflecting the strands of holiday lights Flora Macara and her husband had hung along the roofline of the Inn and the stone walls that skirted the tavern courtyard. A reminder that Christmas would bring Cait no joy this year once she heard her father's news.

Something of his thoughts must have registered in his expression. She raised her chin and narrowed her eyes, but instead of making her fierce, with his coat draped over her shoulders, the body language only made her seem smaller and more fragile.

"Well?" she demanded. "You've obviously got something to say. Get on with it, and stop gaping at me as if I've grown two heads."

"You need to go see your father. Make him tell you the truth—make him listen—and when you're through, if you need me, call me. Whatever's happened between us, I'll be here for you." He couldn't stop himself from moving toward her. Reaching for her. "I've changed, Caitie. You won't believe that, but I'll prove it to you if you'll let me."

She blinked, searched his face. Took a deep, long breath. Then her expression hardened. "You say that while you still reek of whiskey in the middle of the afternoon. Not much has changed, from what I see."

Brice went stiff. "I had half a glass—"

"Like you had with Rhona Grewer before you let

her drag you off to bed? But you know what, it doesn't matter. *You* don't matter. Not to me. Get drunk all day. With anyone you like. Do whatever you like." She stood quietly, spoke quietly, her lip trembling as she said the words.

The lack of sound and fury was far worse than the months when she hung up on him or refused to take his calls. Where there was anger there was hope, but it seemed she'd burned through even that. Convinced herself that what had been between them wasn't worth fighting over. Fighting *for*.

Tired beyond measure, Brice dug in his pocket for the key to the Tea Room. "I don't know why you're so determined to believe the worst about what you saw that day, and I can't change your mind if you won't hear my side of it. But you're wrong about a lot of things, not least that we don't matter to each other. We will always matter. Don't push me away, *mo chridhe*. Don't push away any of the people who want to love you. You're about to find out how much you need us all."

He didn't wait to hear how she would answer. On reaching the Tea Room, he unlocked the door and let himself inside. Cait being back didn't change the fact that he'd promised to finish the painting and remove the FOR SALE sign from the window before Cait saw it. Whatever Cait thought, he wasn't one to break a promise.

Sliding the bolt closed behind himself, he watched her through the glass, waiting to see whether she would try to come in after him. She didn't move, only stood rooted where he'd left her, her face tilted up to the falling snow.

She looked so lost, so broken, he couldn't make himself move away.

Dark House

*"Man is not what he thinks he is,
he is what he hides."*

André Malraux

MORE THAN HIS WORDS, it was Brice's sympathy that scared Cait cold. For as long as she had known him, he'd always hidden deep emotion with attitude or laughter. Watching him stride off toward the Tea Room, she didn't know what to do with the softness she had seen in his expression. The whole conversation made her long to run home to her father and demand to know what was going on.

You didn't win a battle with Donald Fletcher without sufficient ammunition, though, and as her mother had always said: knowledge was the ultimate weapon.

She wished Brice had simply told her what he knew instead of dropping dire hints. It made no sense for him to know anything at all about her father's business, much less to have a key to the Tea Room in his pocket.

Something had changed while she was gone. There was something different about Brice, too, come to that. Aye, he still had the usual faint smudge of grease along the ridge of one sharp cheekbone where he caught it with his thumb as he brushed back his hair. He was still quick enough to anger. But he'd both softened and grown more certain of himself. More tempered. Physically he was leaner, even more gorgeous than she remembered. No less devastating to her equilibrium.

No less infuriating.

God, why had she thought she could bear to come home again?

The previous Christmas with her father in London had been fine. Good. Better than their relationship had ever been before, almost like two grown-up friends. Friends who actually spoke to each other about things that mattered. Or so Cait had believed. Maybe the closeness she'd felt between them had been nothing more than self-delusion, her still trying to fill Robbie's shoes. Now, standing in front of the Tea Room with the wind blowing off the loch and the snow coming down, she felt like a child again, the little sister who would forever run in her brother's shadow. Even when Robbie wasn't there to cast one anymore. Her father had always turned to Robbie when he needed something. Maybe it even made an odd sort of sense that he'd asked Brice for help instead of asking her.

Even as she wondered what Brice was doing for him, Brice moved into the unlit front room, pulled something out of the window, and vanished toward the rear of the building. A moment later, a light shone warmly from the kitchen.

Outside, the wind blew colder. Cait discovered she was shaking, and she burrowed deeper into Brice's coat. It smelled of him, smelled just as she remembered: maleness and grease and the Lava Soap that left his skin clean and pink when he washed his hands. An undertone of automotive leather and a little bit of whiskey. That, too, was familiar.

Too familiar.

Brice had settled his coat around her a hundred times when she was cold. She'd thought she was the only one who wore his clothes. But she'd been wrong.

The weight of the thick black wool threatened to crush her, and she tore the coat off and threw it on the tarmac. She had to fight the temptation to stomp on it, to grind the memories it had brought into the dirty wet asphalt until they lost their power.

Old pain didn't die that easy.

The morning after Brice had asked her to marry him, she'd gone to pull her T-shirt on, but he'd slowly dressed her in his flannel shirt instead, from the bottom up, planting a gentle kiss on the skin beneath each button. She'd worn the shirt and nothing else while they made breakfast together, and the brush of the fabric against her skin had felt like an intimate gesture, something just for her. Only for her. Then the day after Mum's funeral, she'd found Rhona Grewer letting herself out the door of Brice's cottage, her blond hair unaccustomedly tousled and the beautiful blue button-down shirt that Cait had bought Brice for his birthday tied up loosely over a skirt that fit like a second skin.

Being Rhona, she had smiled without a hint of shame. "He's a good man, that one," she'd said, clicking past Cait in her four-inch heels. "Don't take your eyes off him too long, or you might find he's moved on to someone else."

Cait gave herself a shake. Turning her back, she walked past the posh new Land Rover that Brice was driving and slipped into the driver's seat of her own Mini. She couldn't help wondering who the Land Rover belonged to. Had Brice already taken up with someone new?

The thought made Cait feel faintly sick as she slipped back behind the wheel. It reminded her, too, that she really needed to get rid of the car that he'd restored for her. Make a clean break of it. She'd started to advertise the Mini a half-dozen times since she'd moved to London, but she'd never managed to carry through. Selling it would be like selling a piece of herself.

Bone tired, she put her fingers through the grating of the cat carrier where Mrs. Bogan had started to meow what sounded like the first note of a funeral dirge, over and over again. "Hush, now," Cait told her. "I know just how you feel, love. I do. I hear you, and I am sorry I left you so long."

Not in the least soothed by the apology, Mrs. Bogan hissed and dropped into a sulky crouch at the bottom of the carrier. Cait switched the ignition with her hand shaking and reversed back out onto the road.

The car park at the Inn had already started filling up for the evening. A young couple hurried up the path toward the sprawling building as Cait drove past, and the door swung open with a glow of yellow light. Music spilled outside: a bagpipe playing the first notes of "Wild Rover," then drums and an accordion joining in. Voices, too, still sufficiently in tune and tempo to suggest the night was young and the beer had only recently started flowing.

Not so very long ago, Cait would have been in there with everyone else, her back braced against Brice's broad chest, his arms held fast and warm around her, his lips coming down now and again at the end of a song to kiss her hair. He had a fine voice, did Brice. Better than Cait's own, though she'd been the one to sing in the choir.

She put her foot down on the accelerator, suddenly desperate to get home. To hell with the posted limit. She drove straight through the intersection and continued up the hill past the newly rebuilt Village Hall, past the double row of white harled stone houses with warm lights filtering through lace-curtained windows. Eventually, she turned into a long track that led to the house where she'd grown up. But at the top of the drive, she stopped, her hands tight on the wheel.

As with the Tea Room, her mum's absence was unmistakable. No glittering holiday lights dripped like icicles beneath the eaves of the house. No handmade ornaments of gold and silver bells and moons and stars hung on the holly tree beside the door. The porch light was off and, through the picture window at the front, only the pale blue flickering light of the television lit the sitting room.

Cait eased her foot off the brake and let the car

glide down the remainder of the drive. Once she'd parked and turned the ignition off, she left her cases in the boot and took nothing with her except the cat carrier and the small holdall with the box of chocolates she'd brought her father.

The front door was locked, and that was different, too. She stooped to retrieve the key from beneath the flowerpot by the holly tree, but found it wasn't there and had to resort to finding her own among the dozen on her keyring. She couldn't remember the last time she'd had to use it.

Stepping inside, she paused and listened on the threshold. Apart from the low murmur of the television, the house was silent. If her father was home, he didn't seem to have noticed the flash of her headlights as she approached. She tiptoed through the hall and turned into the sitting room, the faint sense of dread she'd been feeling no longer faint at all.

Half-covered in a blanket, her father lay snoring quietly on the sofa. Crumpled wrappers, dirty plates, empty glasses, and a half empty bottle of Scotch littered the low table beside him, but amid the mess, there was something emptier about the remainder of the room.

It took Cait a moment to process that it was physically emptier.

She switched on the lights for a closer look. A bare spot on the wall showed an unfaded square of wallpaper where a painting of the blue-roofed village on Santorini had hung the last time Cait had seen the room—her mother had always dreamed of going there. That wasn't the only bare spot. The blown-up photo of Cait with her mum at university graduation had also gone, along with the portrait of Robbie in his army uniform with the pressed poppy Mum had slipped into the corner, and the framed family photographs that once covered the entire mantle were missing, too. Absent, also, was the carved marble chessboard that had held pride of place on the little Queen Anne table. Her mum's knitting box. The little porcelain figurines from the table beside the sofa. Most of the books from off the shelves.

Every trace of Cait's mother had been stripped away.

The cold tightness in Cait's chest slid deeper, settling in the pit of her stomach and leaving her feeling as empty as the room. She crossed over to the sofa and stood looking down at her father, wondering what to say. The realization that he seemed old, suddenly—and frail and thin—struck her like another body blow. Where was the giant of a man who had loomed over her family all her life?

Had it truly been a year since she'd seen him?

It was an easy day's drive up from London, but she hadn't made the effort. She hadn't allowed herself to make it.

What sort of a daughter did that make her?

Easing herself down to the edge of the sofa beside him, Cait gave his shoulder a gentle shake. "Dad? Wake up."

He stirred and groaned, smacked his lips a time or two, then pulled the blanket toward his chin.

"Wake up, Dad. I'm home."

This time his eyes finally opened. He blinked slowly, then struggled to sit up. "Caitie? What are you doing here? You're not meant to come until tomorrow."

"I decided to drive straight up this morning—I was worried," she said, "and it seems I was right. Look at this place. It's a tip. And look at yourself. What have you been doing?"

He ran a hand through gray hair that seemed sparser than she remembered. Sparser and longer, and where had the whiskers come from?

Slumping back against the cushions, he twitched the blanket back across his feet. "Less of the parental tone of voice if you please, my girl. I'll not be having you lecture me in my own house."

"I wouldn't need to lecture if you'd tell me what

was going on. Something's clearly wrong."

"Nothing a bit of rest won't fix. I've been working too hard, that's all."

Cait pushed to her feet and swallowed down the obvious rebuttal. She retrieved Mrs. Bogan from the cat carrier instead, then crossed back to the picture window with the little warm body pressed tight against her chest. Mrs. Bogan purred loudly, not a contented purr, a nervous one—as if she sensed Cait's frustration—and Cait relaxed her hold and rubbed the cat behind the ears.

Only when she could trust herself again, did she finally look her father in the eye. "I stopped at the Tea Room on my way here," she said. "Since you'd told me you couldn't afford to close the place, I assumed that was where I'd find you."

He swung his legs off the sofa and fumbled for a cane that lay beside him on the floor. His right foot was encased in a walking cast, his sock-clad toes peeking out the open front, and even leaning on the cane, he swayed lightly as if it was hard to balance his large, ungainly frame. "I decided to close the Tea Room early," he said sullenly, not looking at her. "I don't have to be there all the time."

"You haven't been there in a good long while, judging by the state of it. How long has it been since it's been open? And why does Brice have a key?"

"Because I felt like giving him one. Enough questions. I'm tired, so I'm going up to bed. We can talk this over in the morning."

"Brice said I needed to make you tell me what's going on."

Her father exhaled sharply. "Brice's mouth moves faster than his mind. Always has. Should have known better than to trust him with anything."

"Why did you? You've always hated him."

"Because you weren't here."

Cait felt the blow land, but shook it off. "Nice try, but I know your tricks. You're the one who told me I needed to leave the glen, and you've been lying to keep me from finding out whatever you are hiding. Now you're trying to distract me, and you're scaring me instead. Tell me the truth."

"You're making a fuss where none is needed. All right, if you must know, I did a bit more than sprain my ankle. If I'd told you it was broken, you'd have tried to come home, and I didn't want you doing that. Only what with having to take it easy on the leg and Mairi quitting and Kirsty due to have her baby soon—"

"Mairi quit?" Cait stared at him.

A flush crept over his cheekbones. "Said keeping up the library was too much for her. She's gone soft in the head. And don't go listening to her. There's nothing wrong with my temper, whatever she claims."

Cait laughed at that. "No, nothing at all. Not a single thing."

"Anyway, it seemed like the perfect time to spruce the place up. Brice is always looking for money, so I hired him to do some painting. Blame him if you want to blame anyone. He should have finished long since."

"So that's all you're doing? Painting?"

"Aye, I told you."

"Where are the bookshelves then? And where are all Mum's things here at home? Where'd you put them?"

"What are you asking me questions for? We needed to see the walls to paint them, didn't we?" Her father snatched a medicine bottle up off the table and slipped it in his pocket. "This is exactly why I don't tell you anything, if you must know. You're always poking your nose in where it isn't needed. I am still your father, Cait. I can paint what I bloody well want to paint." He released a sigh. Shaking his head, he hobbled slowly, painfully, toward the corridor leaning on his cane.

Cait trailed him to the stairs, feeling helpless, trying to think of something to say that wouldn't make things worse between them. He stopped briefly on the bottom step. "You should get some rest yourself. You've had a long drive. And I don't know why you had to bring that stupid cat. See you keep her away from me, at least."

He climbed the stairs, looking more like an old man than like the father Cait had loved and hated and feared—a little—for the best part of her life.

She wanted to go and shake him. Instead, she lowered her arms so Mrs. Bogan could jump silently to the floor, and she ran up to hug him on the steps. He felt frail in her arms, as though he'd lost half of himself somewhere along the way these past months since Mum had gone.

It was possible, Cait had to acknowledge it, that looking like a fool in her father's eyes might have been part of the reason she hadn't argued when he'd urged her to go to London that day after her mother's funeral. As often as she'd defended Brice, insisted that she loved him, as long as Brice had been the bone of contention that had driven a wedge between them, the idea that she had been wrong all along and her father had been right, had made it easier to agree when he'd insisted she should leave.

"I love you," she whispered, deciding there and then that whatever was going on, she wasn't going to abandon him again.

He put his big paw of a hand on her hair, let it rest there a moment, trembling, then dropped it back down to his side. "I've missed you, Caitie girl. But I never asked you to come home. I wish you had stayed away."

DUMBSTRUCK

"What should I do
about the wild and the tame?
The wild heart that wants to be free,
and the tame heart that
wants to come home."

JEANNETTE WINTERSON

W HILE MRS. BOGAN WAS BUSY GOBBLING, in a most unladylike fashion, the last bit of a dried-out piece of salmon from the fridge, Cait fetched her cases from the boot of the car and lugged them upstairs. In her old room, she pulled an old-favorite stretched-out fisherman's sweater from the box of discards beneath the bed and paired that with black leggings and heavy socks to ward off the chill that had settled in the house. Then she headed back downstairs.

The kitchen smelled of smoked fish, dust, and

disuse. Even the clean dishes in the drying rack had dried specks of food on them and that greasy, not-quite-clean feeling when she ran a thumb across them. By the look of it, nothing in the house had been given more than a cursory wipe-down in months. As much to burn off the confused emotions that were spinning through her like electricity as anything else, Cait dug out the cleaning supplies to give the place a proper turn-out.

After rewashing the dishes, she cleaned out the near-empty refrigerator and wiped down the baseboards and cabinets. But like the rest of the house, her father had stripped the kitchen of anything that had belonged to her mum—or that her mum had cared about. The more places Cait looked, the more things she found missing. Even the book of recipes handed down generation to generation in her mother's family was gone from its customary place on the little bookshelf in the corner.

Cait wiped the dust from the telephone directory, which was the only remaining book. And suddenly the unanswered questions were more than she could bear. How was she supposed to sleep? Though it felt much later, the wall clock assured her it was only half past eight, so she flung down the dust cloth and pulled a heavy coat from the hook by the kitchen door. Then realizing she had no shoes, she ran upstairs to get them and to collect the keys to the Mini as well.

Driving along the loch road to Elspeth Murray's Breagh House, she told herself she would knock only if it looked as though Elspeth were awake. But of course, even if she'd retired to bed already, Elspeth wouldn't be sleeping yet. Elspeth always had been a night owl, and she was likely to be working downstairs in the section of the house that she'd converted into a museum of Highlands history. Fake Highlands history, usually, though well intentioned. Most of the items Elspeth claimed to have belonged to Rob Roy MacGregor or the Revered Robert Kirk or other historical figures from the glen were pure fabrication on her part. For all that, though, Elspeth knew the deep-down truth of human nature better than anyone else in Balwhither. If anything in the village was ever worth knowing, Elspeth Murray would be the one who knew it.

Pulling the Mini to a stop in the circular drive of the Gothic revival house that had belonged to the Murrays for several centuries, Cait took stock of the building. Lights inside, and still more all along the flower beds forming a welcoming path from the edge of the drive to the wide front steps, suggested that Elspeth was still awake.

Elspeth's was one of Cait's favorite houses in the

glen. These days, it was second in size only to Connal MacGregor's Inverlochlarig House that sat in stone splendor a short way down the road at the far end of Loch Daoine, the smaller and more distant of the glen's two lakes. But across the water, on the opposite shore, the ruined Stewart house had once been slightly larger, and so had the old Fletcher home that had become the Library and Tea Room. Wandering through Elspeth's rooms as a child, Cait used to imagine what it would be like to live in a place this grand, where Highland chieftains used to meet to discuss war or cattle raids and beautifully-dressed women had come to dance.

It struck Cait abruptly that all things crumbled. Buildings. Families. The old Stewart home was a crumbling ruin and, aside from Mad Mackenzie, the Stewarts themselves were gone. With Robbie dead, her father was the last of the Balwhither Fletchers, too.

Cait had left him in the glen alone.

She swung out of the car and took a deep breath of air that smelled of nothing except peat and soil and water. No exhaust fumes or gasoline stench. No restaurant waste rotting in the dumpsters behind the corner pub near her London flat. The glen smelled wild as the wind, and lonely.

"You coming in, then?" Elspeth Murray called from the top of the steps. "Or d'you plan to stand out here all night and catch your death?"

Cait hadn't noticed the door opening, but seeing Elspeth standing there, her feet launched themselves down the path of their own volition. Feeling Elspeth's arms wrap around her, she allowed herself to be gathered into the warmth and comfort, and somehow it made her lonelier still. She'd missed this. The simple connection of someone holding her. Embracing her.

But she wasn't going to cry. She wasn't the type to cry.

"Och, you let it all out," Elspeth said, patting her back. "I can feel you holding the weight of the world inside you as though it will all come crashing down if you ease yourself an inch. Is this what they've done to you down in London?"

"I was all right in London. It's being home that's done it," Cait said, drawing back.

Elspeth, dressed in a dark blue sweater, a pale tweed skirt, and oversized bedroom slippers in place of her usual sturdy shoes, was the only person Cait had seen in the glen so far who seemed entirely unchanged. Her gray curls were still chin length, no lighter or darker than Cait remembered, and even with the gray days that shrouded the Highlands in December, her cheeks were still pink and weathered from walking the track to the village and back each day. Most of all, she wore her listening face, the silent promise of a willing ear and as much—or as little— advice as someone wished.

She grasped Cait by the elbow and pulled her inside. "Come on inside, poor love. I'll put the kettle on, and I've got some pastries that Brando's Emma brought over from the hotel this morning. You haven't met her yet, but she's American—like my niece. Brando found her in Cornwall, of all places, when he went to his sister Janet's wedding, and as long as we've all been taking bets on when some girl would snatch him up, none of us saw that coming. They'll be getting married next summer. Another lovely wedding in the glen. But before I go getting pastries, have you had your supper? I could easily fix you something."

"Honestly, I haven't much of an appetite at all."

Inside the house, the stained-glass windows and the chandelier suspended from the ceiling in the foyer were a far cry from Cait's much simpler home, all those things having been left behind when the Tea Room was converted. Still, like Cait's mum, Elspeth had a knack for making the place seem warm and inviting. She shuffled to the kitchen sink to fill the kettle, and Cait flopped down in the chair at the table by the wall. Briefly, she bit her lip, trying to decide where to begin. But her mother had always taught her that for any difficult conversation, it was best to start at the beginning and come straight to the point.

She folded her hands on the table. "What's wrong with my father?" she asked. "He's been telling me he's fine, and he clearly isn't."

"He hasn't explained?" Elspeth slapped the water off and turned. "Even now that you're home?"

"Explained what? I saw a medicine bottle on the table, and the house is a proper mess. And I know he's renovating the Tea Room. What I can't fathom is why, and Brice—the knob head—refused to tell me."

Elspeth's lips tightened. Her chest rose and fell again deeply, and she crossed to the stove to set the kettle on the burner. "It isn't Brice's fault, though he's no different than Donald when it comes to things like pride and promises. Of course, you know a thing or two about pride yourself, don't you? Well, perhaps we all do, come to that."

"You're not exactly speaking plainly," Cait said.

Sighing again, Elspeth came to sit in the chair beside Cait's and covered Cait's hand with her own where it lay on the scarred wooden table. "Your father has bone cancer, Cait. None of us knew until this morning when I ran into Brice. We'd all thought he'd fallen and broken his leg, but it was cancer that caused the break."

Cancer. The word echoed in Cait's ears until the peal of it had set her muscles trembling. She hadn't let her thoughts wander in that direction yet. Hadn't dared to. She'd thought her father's arthritis must have gotten worse, or heart problems, a dozen other things, but mostly it had been the obvious signs of depression that had worried her when she saw him.

Cancer? She couldn't take that in.

Not when the ugliness of the disease had stolen her mother away already.

"How bad?" she asked with her mouth gone so dry that the words were indistinct.

"Bad, love." Elspeth's answer was flat. "From what I gather, he put the pain down to arthritis and didn't bother going to the doctor until he stepped wrong and the leg fractured—"

"He only told me he had twisted an ankle. Claimed it was nothing to worry about," Cait said, shivering again as her body temperature dropped.

"Aye, well. We knew he'd broken it—he admitted that much. But he locked himself in the cottage and sent everyone packing when they tried to help. This morning was the first we'd heard about the cancer, and I only know because he had no choice but to confess to Brice once he knew you were coming home."

"No choice? I don't understand," Cait said.

"Brice had thought he could have the work done

long ago, but he's had a project he's been working on that he needs to finish by Christmas, and he didn't think the Tea Room was much of a rush. I suppose he hoped Donald would come to his senses, too, anyway. Then with you on your way back, your father rang and begged Brice to make it look like the place wasn't closed. Brice refused, and to get him to agree, Donald finally told him the truth. And before you ask, Brice had already promised to stay out of any business between you and your father before he found out Donald hadn't been telling you the truth. Until this morning, I haven't seen him as furious over anything since the day you left the glen."

"But why didn't anyone think to call me when Dad broke his leg? I would have come home."

"We thought you knew. He said you did. Said you were busy with your job and he didn't want you having to put that aside to come back and nurse him. And he's been full of himself as a young bull about how well you're doing at the newspaper—he shows everyone every article that's got your name on it. As if we haven't all been keeping up ourselves. He's proud of you, you know."

Cait shrugged that off. If he was, he'd never said as much to her. All she could think of were the lies that had piled up through the months. The way he'd kept her in London deliberately. Kept her away from him. She couldn't help thinking that he wouldn't have done that to her brother. He'd have told Robbie what was wrong.

Robbie would have known.

She felt dizzy with the thousands of questions swirling around her brain. "What about treatment for the cancer? What have the doctors said?"

Elspeth rose as the kettle began to whistle, but paused briefly to squeeze Cait's shoulder in reassurance. "From what he told Brice this morning, your father doesn't see the point of chemo and radiation when they'd only prolong the end a little while. I'm sorry, love. You know how stubborn the man can be. You might phone the doctor yourself and see if he'll talk to you. That'd be my advice. That and a cuppa with a good dose of sugar for the shock of it. I can't help you with the first, but I'll have the tea for you in just a tick."

Needles of ice laced Cait's blood, and her hands and feet felt numb.

Elspeth went and switched the kettle off, then shifted to the refrigerator to get a pastry box and set it on the table. With her usual efficiency, she had the box open and an intricately braided miniature apple shortbread tart served up on a plate before Cait could even protest. "Here, eat this. You need some sugar. If you get any more pale, we'll lose you in the snow outside."

"Why Brice? What's he doing with the Tea Room? Why would my father bother with any of that with everything that's going on—and why would Brice want to help him?"

Cait broke off a corner of the pastry and crumbled it listlessly between her fingers. "What about the Tea Room, then? What's the point of painting with all this going on?" Then she paused and looked up, her tone bitter as she said the obvious, "Oh, I've been stupid, haven't I? He's not fixing it up at all. He means to sell it."

"Don't blame Brice for that, either." Elspeth finished pouring the hot water into to the teapot and turned with the steaming kettle in her hand. "Your father told him you knew all about that, too. Said he wanted to sell the place and start thinking about moving down to London to be closer to you. No one questioned that—Donald hadn't been able to keep up with the place even before he broke his leg." Elspeth released a sigh. "Honestly, I could strangle that man. Morag should have done it years ago. If I'd been here myself, I might have figured things out sooner, but I've been in America with my sister these last three months—she's finally getting divorced—and I've only just gotten back."

Cait couldn't wrap her head around it all. "Does everyone believe I wouldn't have come back? I wouldn't have just left him—"

"Shh, love. Don't be hard on yourself. Or him. Your mum was Donald's rudder the most past of his life. He doesn't know what to do without her. Then, too, you know how pigheaded he can be. We've all let him down. We left everything to Brice, since he seemed to be the only one Donald would let in the house."

"Why?" Kate glanced at her sharply. "And why would Brice even want to help?"

Elspeth's expression softened. "I suspect you can answer the last question for yourself if you give it any thought. As for your father, who can tell what's going on in his head? Maybe it gives him pleasure to see Brice running ragged, working all hours in the garage then trying to put in time at the Tea Shop on top of it, painting and carting the books away to the consignment shops—"

"The books, too?" Cait felt a knot of something cold and hard building and building in her chest.

Elspeth set down the kettle and brought the teapot to the table. "Your father insists he wants it all put back the way it was before your mum began the library. I can see his point. We've had more tourists coming and staying lately, but not so many yet that folks are clamoring to buy businesses in the glen. It'd be hard enough for your dad to sell up as a restaurant. No one from outside's going to understand how important the library is to the glen—or be willing to spend the time or money trying to run it. Once Brice finishes with it, it could be sold as a house or a shop or a restaurant—whatever someone might want it for."

Cait straightened slowly from her chair. It was all too much to process.

Only two things she knew for certain. She couldn't go back to London with her father sick, and she couldn't let the Library and Tea Room close.

Not only had the library been her mother's passion, it was important to the glen. With the nearest public library too far for most to travel, there wasn't a child in Balwhither who hadn't discovered the magic of reading from a book Cait's mother had picked out for them. The fact that her father was willing to throw that away, and the fact that Brice MacLaren had gone along with the idea, made Cait want to throttle them both. And Brice had not only done that, he'd tried to hide it from her. That was almost worse than anything else he'd ever done.

Simple Words

*"One day I will find the right words,
and they will be simple."*

JACK KEROUAC
THE DHARMA BUMS

T HE FROSTY TEMPERATURE OUTSIDE made it impossible to open the windows, but Brice was used to paint fumes. He cranked the heat up to help the paint dry faster and set to work. What he needed, though, was a pot of coffee—the days of working twelve hours straight trying to finish up the Aston Martin on top of squeezing in time helping Donald with the Tea Room renovation had begun to take their toll. Yawning, he forced himself to finish an entire wall so the paint would be even, then he climbed down from the stepladder and headed back to the kitchen to make himself a pot.

The phone rang as he emptied the old filter, wet grounds dribbling across his shoes as well as the floor and counter. He dug his mobile out of his pocket and groaned when he saw that it was Donald Fletcher. "What now, Donald?"

"Is Cait there with you?" Donald's voice was uneven with a note of panic.

"Why would Cait be here?"

"Because she isn't *here*. Where else would she be? She came home early. The bloody phone was downstairs, so I had to wait until she'd gone to bed before I could ring to warn you. Then I discovered her car was gone."

"She could have driven off somewhere to think. You know how she gets. And I hope you've come to your senses and told her the truth." Brice tore a paper towel off the roll and used it to wipe the floor.

"I've no intention of telling Cait anything, so long as you do your part. I won't have her worrying herself to death for whatever time I've got left. She's been through that with her mum already. Now did you get that FOR SALE sign taken down?"

"Aye, but I wish you'd change your mind. It's cruel, what you're doing to her. Cruel, and it will only make her furious, and hurt. That's the long and short of it. You're going to hurt her, keeping all these

52

secrets, and that's what she'll remember about you as she lays you in the grave."

"You're a fine one to talk about hurting her. Anyway, it's my own business what I tell her, and I'll thank you to keep your head right out of it. Though when you've ever kept your head around our Cait, I can't remember. But that's the point. She's a Fletcher. I don't want her staying here in the glen, throwing herself away—throwing away her education and her talent—on the likes of you. She's finally making something of her life, which is more than I allowed for her mother or for Robbie. Now Cait's all I've got left, and I'm determined to see her right."

"You're all she's got left, too, you ruddy great fool. Did you ever think of that?"

Donald growled, his voice deep and sounding momentarily more like his old self. "Don't you think you can talk to me like that, Brice MacLaren. I'm doing this for her—and don't forget you promised you wouldn't say a word. I'll not have you trying to worm your way back into her life the way you've tried to win me over. Come the new year, she'll be off back to London if I have to drive her there myself."

In his usual autocratic way, Donald rang off without a good-bye, as if he were the king of the world and everyone else his vassals. But that had always been Donald's biggest problem with Cait. She didn't take well to being told what to do, not for anything. Not if you happened to value your piece of mind.

Wishing he'd never made the mistake of promising to stay out of Donald's relationship with his daughter, Brice tossed the phone down onto the tarp-covered table behind him harder than he'd intended. It landed with a smack and bounced to the floor, and when he reached past a chair that had been left askew, he found that the screen had cracked. The chair slid, and as he scrambled to keep his balance, he banged his head on the underside of the table. He flung the chair aside harder than he'd meant to, and it banged into the wall hard enough to leave a dent in the newly painted surface. A dent he was going to have to repair and paint again.

Fists clenched, Brice fought to regain his self-control. He'd tried so hard to be done with anger, and yet here he was again, breaking things instead of mending them. That was just like him, wasn't it? His own worst enemy. No matter how hard he worked, no matter how hard he tried to be better, it always felt like an uphill battle.

He separated a fresh coffee filter from the ruffled stack and fitted it into the stainless-steel machine on the counter, then he fetched ground beans from the refrigerator, measured them out, and added water.

The machine spit and sputtered as it began to brew, and while he waited for the coffee to drip, he realized Donald Fletcher had set him up good and proper when it came to Cait. Risked ruining everything Brice had been hoping for. And if—in the deep recesses of his mind—Brice had ever thought that helping Donald would make the stubborn old tyrant soften toward him, he'd long since learned that he'd been mistaken.

Nothing softened Donald Fletcher, not even the prospect of facing death. Since Morag's passing, Donald had managed to drive most everyone in the glen away, and not even the offers of help when he'd broken his ankle had kept him from being surly.

It might have been different if Elspeth had been around. Elspeth Murray would have noticed he wasn't leaving his house or going to the Tea Room, and she wouldn't have been deterred by Donald growling that he didn't want a fuss. She'd have done exactly what Brice had done, retrieved the key from beneath the flowerpot by the holly tree, seen the state of the place—and the emptiness of the pantry and refrigerator—and taken things in hand herself. Only desperation—and the fact Brice had promised not to say a word to Cait about any of it—had allowed Donald's pride to accept anything Brice had managed to do for him.

Brice should have known the wily old goat hadn't told him the entire story. And once the Tea Room had come into it, promise or no promise, Brice should have confessed to Cait.

As it was, he didn't see how she'd ever forgive him for what he was doing. Never mind for what she thought he'd already done.

Running a calloused hand along the back of his neck, Brice kneaded the rigid muscles as he looked around the kitchen. Gone was the cheery yellow color that Morag had chosen for it, along with the border of heather blossoms that Cait herself had painted. All of the hand-painted borders throughout the house were gone and so were the bookshelves and the books themselves. In Brice's estimation, Donald's "improvements" had stripped away all of the charm that added value, until all that remained of the old Library and Tea Room was a blank canvas of a restaurant with a decent kitchen and a dozen empty rooms with no personality at all.

Unable to stand idle any longer, he got a cup from the cupboard and filled it directly from the stream of coffee descending from the machine, added a bit of milk from the refrigerator, and took a cautious sip as he headed back into the room where he'd been painting. After draining half the milky coffee, he left the cup on the floor, dialed up the volume on Niall Horan's "Slow Hands," which was playing on the radio, and turned the stepladder to the next wall so he could begin cutting in the paint along the ceiling. The combination of the coffee and the strong beat of the music gave him a bit of energy, and he made himself throw his back into the work. That was what he needed to keep from worrying about Cait. Hard work, sweat, and eventually a bit of sleep.

He didn't hear the door open—didn't notice anything but the music and the slap of the paint brush until he bent to load more paint on his brush and saw Cait striding across the floor toward him in the old barn coat of her father's, her face flushed and her hair crackling with temper. He jumped hastily off the stepladder and turned to face her.

"What are you playing at?" she demanded. "Why didn't you call and tell me? Instead you've been helping him for four months. *Four* months! And you couldn't bother to tell me what was going on? Or that he was selling the place?" She stopped in front of him and jabbed her finger into his chest.

"Easy, Cait. I didn't know about the cancer myself until this morning. But would you have taken my call if I'd tried? You didn't return a single message after you left me."

Cait flushed, but then her eyes narrowed, which again was vintage Cait. "All you had to do was mention his broken leg or say he was selling. Or you could have emailed or gotten someone else to phone me."

"None of us knew until this morning that you needed to be told! The old sod said you were busy working. Which was the truth, wasn't it? So far as it went, at least." Easing away from her, Brice started to flick the radio off so they wouldn't have to raise their voices, but then he thought better of it.

Cait needed to shout. He needed to let her shout.

She didn't, though. She went quiet instead. "You knew when you saw me earlier. The whole time we were talking, you knew and you hinted and you kept the truth from me. I'd thought better of you than that, though I don't know why. Lord knows, you can't handle the difficult things. You never could."

He had thought he'd grown past being stung by words, but somehow the people Brice loved best had always managed to hurt him the most. Probably because they were the ones who knew where to strike the hardest blows.

"Hold on, Cait," he said as she turned to leave. Just once, he wished he could find the right words, the perfect words for her. "Your father begged me not to tell you. He begged. I've never seen him like that, so

I promised him I would leave things for the two of you to sort out on your own."

"He was trying to keep you away from me. Obviously. But why were you helping him at all? Why would you help him do *this*?" She waved her hand at the empty room, the pale and lifeless walls. "How could you help him do it when you know what the library meant to my mother? All the time and love she put into this place."

"You left him. Same as you left me. He said you were busy and didn't care—"

"And you *believed* him?" The words were angry, but Cait's chin wobbled, the way it did when she was fighting to be brave, refusing to let the tears come.

Brice couldn't help reaching for her, pulling her into his arms to comfort her, the way he'd done a hundred times. "He didn't have anyone else to help him, love, and he was ready to try doing it all himself. You know how he is. He would have killed himself trying."

She stood rigid in his embrace, but only for a moment. Then the tears came fast and hard, and she burrowed into his chest as if that would muffle the sound and hide the show of weakness. She was like her father in that, how much she hated anyone to see her vulnerable.

In Brice's arms, she felt warm and familiar and *right*. Every muscle, every cell in his skin, remembered the curves and hollows of her, the softness that she tried to hide from everyone. As much as he'd told himself there was no guarantee—no matter how hard he worked or what he managed to achieve—that she would ever come back to him, he had never stopped hoping. He breathed deeply now, memorizing the new scent of her, the shampoo that smelled more sophisticated, the perfume she had never used before.

"I can't lose everything. I can't lose everyone," she said, raising her face to look at him.

"You haven't," he said, hoarsely. "Not everyone."

Briefly, he thought he saw recognition and even a hint of hunger in her eyes, the same hunger that he was feeling. Lowering his head slowly, he gave her time before his lips met hers. He felt the warmth of her breath, barely brushed the pillow softness of her mouth . . .

At the last second, she wrenched away.

"Don't," she said, and her voice was ragged. "What do you think you're doing?"

He didn't know what to tell her. What did she want to hear? What could he possibly say that would make them—the two of them—all right again?

"I'm apologizing, Cait. That was an apology

kiss." He caught both her hands and brought them against his chest. "You know I've never been good with words. I've made mistakes, a lot of them, but I'm hoping you'll forgive me, or at least hear me out. Give me the chance to tell you what happened that day. Let me show you I am changing."

Moments, long and tense moments, went by. Her expression softened slowly, as if the anger she'd been bottling up was finally seeping away. Then she pulled her hands away from his and raised one to briefly cup his cheek.

"I can't. Especially not after you helped my father lie to me," she said.

COWARDICE

*"It took a queer sort of courage
to admit to cowardice..."*

GEORGE R. R. MARTIN
A GAME OF THRONES

C AIT HAD EXAMINED HER OWN BEHAVIOR a thousand times, every stupid thing she'd ever done. She'd been willful and naive and defiant at times in her life. She'd been selfish, too. Until this moment as she turned away from Brice and rushed toward the door, she had never knowingly been a coward. Even so, she had to admit that it was cowardice that made her run from him, that kept her from kissing him the way her heart and body longed to kiss him despite her better judgement.

How could he still make her feel like this? He had only to look at her, to touch her, and she forgot all common sense, forgot that she had more important things to think about than an attraction that refused to die.

She couldn't let herself forget. Not for a single minute.

Only when she was safely near the doorway and well out of reach did she stop and look back. He was still watching her, his face raw with the little boy loneliness that had made her fall in love with him in the first place.

She couldn't let that stop her. "I won't let him sell this place," she said. "The glen needs the library, so I need you to put everything back. The shelves, the books, the paint. Everything."

He moved toward her with the brush in his hand, the overhead lamps casting his shadow ahead of him on the old wooden floor. "It's too late for that. The stencils you and your mother painted are already painted over in most of the rooms. I'm sorry, Cait. The painting's nearly finished, and I've taken the shelves and the books down to the consignment fair in Edinburg. I know for a fact the shelves have sold already—someone bought half of them before I even got the final lot delivered."

The blows just kept coming. More of the things Cait's mother had done, things they had done together, simply vanished as if they'd never been.

And the books? Her mum had found a lot of them at charity shops and jumble sales, scrounging up donations from everyone she met. She'd chosen every book she put on the shelves because she knew there would be someone particular in the glen who would love it. And she hadn't merely taken the jacket copy or the word of reviewers as gospel, either. She had read each book herself, or skimmed it at least.

Cait's father had known all that. Of all people, he knew how much love his wife had poured into the library.

How could Brice have helped him do this?

Cait's jaw set with determination. "You'll have to find those books and bring them back. I don't care what you have to do to make that happen. The shelves aren't as important. If you can get them, too, then so much the better, but if not, just find me shelves to replace them. And stop at the paint shop while you're at it so we can get rid of all this white. Are you hearing what I'm saying? You helped create this mess, and you're going to help me put everything back the way it was." Her voice cracked, and she set her teeth. "This isn't a favor I'm asking. I'll pay you for the work, and whatever you have to do to buy everything back again, I'll pay you for that, too."

It was a fine, brave speech, and she was proud of

it. So why did she feel like she was begging?

Because Brice was looking at her with pity.

"You don't need the old bookshelves," he said.

"I already said that—"

"No. I mean, I don't need to find you *any* bookshelves. I'll make built-ins for you." His voice was soft enough that she could barely hear it over the pounding music. "I know where I can get my hands on shelving, and built-ins would make the rooms look bigger. Better."

"I don't want better!" Cait's nails dug half-moons into her palms. "I just want what was here," she added more quietly. "It's all there is left of my mother. There's nothing else."

"Wait!" Brice called as she walked toward the door.

She stopped. "What?"

His footsteps creaked toward her, heavy and uneven. Uncharacteristically uncertain. "I didn't do this to hurt you, Cait. You have to know that. Whatever's between us, I wouldn't hurt you."

Her back was so stiff the muscles ached. Every fiber, every corner of her ached. "I used to think you wouldn't, but I found out the hard way that I was wrong. You can tell yourself you were only doing all this to help my father, but you had to know how much I'd hate it. You had to know it *would* hurt. Why didn't you think to ask me?"

"I made a mistake. We all make mistakes. You could have asked me about what happened with Rhona, for instance. Listened when I tried to tell you. You were supposed to trust me."

"I was going to marry you—"

"Were you?" He took a step closer. "Really? Until death us do part and for all the right reasons? Cait, if you trusted me enough to spend the rest of your life with me, you would have heard me out when I told you there was nothing between me and Rhona. Nothing happened. You would have believed me. Believed *in* me."

"Which *you* was I meant to believe in, Brice? The sober one or the one you are after you've been drinking? You never denied you'd been drinking with her that afternoon. The day after I buried my mother."

"All right, yes. That was stupid. I meant to have a glass with her and one turned into more. But you know me. You knew that about me. I've never pretended to be anyone but who I am."

"And maybe I finally realized that being who you were, it was only a matter of time before I lost you," Cait said, the words catching in her throat so that they came out sounding thin and cold. "I couldn't afford to lose anyone else."

Sudden tears made her eyes sting.

She hadn't meant to say that, didn't even know that was how she'd felt. But that was the way of truth, it could sneak up sometimes the way wildcats could slink out of the darkness, as if they'd appeared from nothing. Cait hadn't left the glen because she'd been angry at Brice, she realized. She'd left because it hurt too much to lose the people that she loved.

Seeing Rhona wearing Brice's shirt that afternoon, seeing the bottle and glasses on the kitchen table, the rumpled sheets, had made her realize she couldn't count on him. Made her see that she'd taken him for granted, and that she could still lose him to drinking or another woman.

Her father had always told her she couldn't count on Brice, that Brice wasn't the sort of man anyone could count on.

Clearly, that much hadn't changed. And Brice wasn't defending himself. He stood looking at her, his face shuttered and his Adam's apple rising and falling as if he was swallowing words he didn't want to say. The paint-splattered black T-shirt he wore fit tight over his chest and arms, and she'd been wrong before when she'd thought that he looked leaner. Only his face had sharpened. The rest of him was more muscled than it had been. Harder, as though he'd been punishing himself with the weights. The lamplight played over sharp cheekbones and darkened his eyes, deepened the creases between his nose and mouth. Cait wanted to trace her fingers over every inch of that face, relearn the lines of it, but that was dangerous. *He* was dangerous—and exciting. And untrustworthy. Unstable.

Sobered by the reminder, she wrapped her arms around her waist, holding herself in. Steeling herself. "Please, find the books and get them back for me. Get me some shelves. That's all I want. I don't need this to be one of your I'll-get-to-it-next-week projects that stretch out six months. I'd like to get the place back up and running as quickly as possible and show Dad that I can manage."

"I'll do what I can. I promise. And I am sorry. Truly." He offered her a weak echo of one of his old rakish grins, but she saw that she'd hurt him again— and again she hadn't meant to. Her tongue seemed to be running away with her tonight.

That was another reason she needed to get away from him. Far away. Even as she turned back toward the door, though, she found herself asking another question. "Does everyone here blame me for not coming back when Dad broke his leg?"

"You shouldn't care what they think."

"Of course I care. We're not twelve anymore, or

sixteen, or even twenty. The glen's too small to live here with people talking about us behind our backs. It's a community, and we have to be part of it. Both of us. That's the thing you never understood when I came back from university. Maybe it takes leaving this place to see that for all the way everyone meddles and interferes, the way they all know everything someone's done before they've even done it, that's better than living where no one cares at all."

Brice's eyes fastened on hers, searching for answers Cait didn't have herself. "Are you thinking of staying for good, then?"

The way he looked at her, as if he saw her, as if he liked her no matter how ugly she felt inside, had always been her downfall.

"I'll stay at least as long as my father needs me," she said. "Which means you and I will need to find a way to get along. Can you do that?"

"You're the last person in the world I'd ever want to hurt, *mo ghràdh*. I'll do whatever I can to make things right."

DARKNESS

C AIT HAD FORGOTTEN HOW MANY STARS shone above the Highlands, so bright that when she lay sleepless in her bed, she could almost hear them whispering an invitation through the window. She had missed them, and she had missed the brilliant moon that gilded the surface of the lochs and sparkled like diamonds on the crisp, cold snow. She'd always felt sorry for people who spent so much time yearning for what they wanted that they didn't take time to appreciate what they had. Was she any better, though?

She'd been so focused on what she'd lost that she hadn't looked around to discover how much she had left.

Used to waking up early in London, this far north the stars were still out when she rose and dressed in jeans and three layers of soft wool sweaters. Carrying her shoes and jacket, and trailed by a grumpy Mrs. Bogan, she padded along the corridor in thick hiking socks and stopped by the closed door of her father's room. No sound came from within, so she eased the door gently open.

In the moonlight pouring through the window, she had no trouble seeing. It was harder to believe her eyes. Where the old sleigh bed that her mum and dad had restored together should have been, there was only empty flooring—the whole room was empty, save for her father asleep on a pile of blankets in the corner. Even the clothing of her father's that had once been stored in the heavy Jacobean dresser now lay in neat stacks on the floor, and not a stick of furniture remained.

Her father had missed his calling. He should have been an actor. Cait's heart squeezed when she thought about the telephone conversations in which he told her about the tourists who'd come into the Tea Room and given her the latest news from the glen as though nothing in the world was wrong.

He literally had gotten rid of everything that had any connection to Cait's mum, as if he couldn't bear to face a single memory. The house, the Tea Room, everything he'd done was like a sharp steel blade tearing through Cait's heart.

Muscles locking in place on another thought, she inhaled sharply, then pulled the door closed and ran on tiptoes to the room that had been her brother's. Her mother had kept all of Robbie's things in place, and Cait had found her in here sometimes, sitting on his bed. Cait would sit beside her and take her hand, neither of them saying a word until, fifteen minutes or a half-hour later, Cait's mother would finally stand up and smile a little tremulously. Then they would leave, and Cait's mother would shut the door, and neither of them would bring it up.

Afraid she'd find Robbie's room empty, too, Cait hesitated with her hand on the door's glass-knobbed handle. Then she steeled herself and went inside.

The fact that all of Robbie's things were still there was almost as shocking as her father's empty room had been. But the air inside was thick and musty, and when she sank onto the edge of the bed where her mother used to sit, the motion sent up a cloud of dust that clogged her throat. Apparently, her father hadn't cleaned the room since Cait had left, and Cait hadn't had time to do more than a cursory clean a good while before that while her mum was ill.

She wanted both to thump her father and to hold him tight. But he wasn't the sort who would accept either of those things.

Where had he been sleeping? In her room, maybe? Or more likely, downstairs on the sofa. It must have been hard for him to even climb the stairs with a broken ankle—hard for him to take care of himself at all.

Her legs felt numb as she got up. She walked over to the photo that Robbie had pinned up on the wall when he'd come home on leave. It showed Robbie and his mates playing football at the base in Afghanistan, and whoever had snapped the pic had caught Robbie kicking the ball into the goal, the ball sailing forward clearly heading between the posts at an angle the goalie couldn't reach. The joy of scoring was already breaking over Robbie's face and the faces of his team.

Cait touched the image lightly and then let herself out of the room with her eyes swimming.

Downstairs, she searched the old back sitting room that her father used as a workroom looking for something that would give her the name of the doctor her father had seen about his cancer. If he couldn't bear to see a stick of furniture that carried memories of her mother, he wasn't likely to let Mum's doctor treat him, either.

The narrow desk beside the settee was a mess. Her father had thrown stacks of unopened mail on it so often that sealed envelopes and catalogs had fallen to the floor beside it. Cait sifted through them, wondering if she dared open the phone and electric bills to see whether he'd been bothering to pay. But there were more pressing matters that the two of them would need to argue over.

It was scarcely half past seven, too early yet to phone anyone, when she finally unearthed a paper from a cancer support center that had the name of a referring physician. And after that it was easy to find the contact information.

She retreated toward the kitchen where Mrs. Bogan was sitting in the doorway, her tail wrapped around her forelegs with the tip twitching. Cait scooped her up and cuddled her, receiving more comfort than she was giving.

"Yes, I know. You're starving," she said, burying her face in Mrs. Bogan's fur.

Mrs. Bogan began to purr, a low, deep rumble, and while Cait closed her eyes and concentrated on the sound, Mrs. Bogan wiggled closer, laying her head in the curve of Cait's shoulder and letting it rest there while her whiskers tickled the skin beneath Cait's chin.

That was the thing about cats. As crotchety and demanding as they might be, they were always there when you needed them. And at that moment, Cait felt like she had no one else at all.

"It's human beings who are the problem," she said, walking into the kitchen still carrying Mrs. Bogan. "Men. They should be required to come with instruction manuals. Not for us, for themselves. Only they wouldn't bother to read them, and women would still be left trying to find the extra screws and leftover pieces and cleaning up the messes they leave behind."

She fed Mrs. Bogan, then set about the task of making breakfast for her father. God only knew how long it had been since he had eaten a proper meal. For all that the refrigerator looked sparse, though, there was a reasonable supply of staples, and she found eggs and butter and milk, along with a package of sausage that looked as though it should still be all right. Her mulish streak urged Cait to make her mother's pancakes, to force her father to remember *something*. She settled for making Aberdeen butteries instead, though she wished she had the recipe book to work from. Maybe even more than the individual library books, that was the biggest loss. Generations of Stewart women had added their best recipes to that book, or appended notes to recipes from older generations about what dish went with another, who in the family particularly loved something, or how another version was worse or better. Sometimes, while her mum was baking, Cait would sit at the table, her legs wrapped around the chair legs reading the notes and imagining the women who had written them.

At eight o'clock on the dot, she phoned the doctor's office, and after a bit of runaround, managed to sweet-talk the receptionist into getting Dr. Webster on the phone. Fully expecting that he would say he couldn't speak to her about her father's condition, she was surprised when there was almost no delay before a brisk, deep voice came on the line.

"I'm told you're on the chart as Donald Fletcher's emergency contact," he said. "I'm relieved to hear from you, to tell you the truth."

"Aye, sir. I've only just found out about the cancer. I don't know much about his treatment."

"I wish he'd let us provide some. We're only focusing on pain management at the moment."

"Which is why I'm calling. I wanted to ask you how much the chemo or radiation would help. I'm sure it's impossible to predict, but before I try and argue with him, it would help to know if we're talking a matter of additional years or only months."

"The surgery's what would buy him time."

"Surgery?" Cait sat down at the kitchen table and stared out the window where the sky was turning lavender and orange as the sun began to rise. "To cut the cancer out of the bone? I didn't realize that was a possibility."

The doctor hesitated. "I'm afraid we're beyond the stage where limb-salvage would be an option, but as I explained to him, a lower limb prosthetic could still provide him full mobility. The longer we wait, the harder and more extensive additional treatment will become, and the more chance there is that the cancer will metastasize."

Cait pressed her free hand against her chest where a combination of elation and anger was making her heart beat faster. "You're saying the condition isn't hopeless if you amputate?"

"I made that clear to him." The other end of the line was silent a moment before the doctor answered. "There are no guarantees, of course, but overall, the five-year survival rate for bone cancer is seventy percent. Your father could have a reasonable expectation for recovery. I'd like to have him in better nutritional condition for the surgery, but frankly it's his attitude that's the problem."

"Meaning his stubbornness is literally going to kill him."

The doctor gave a startled chuckle. "I wish I could say he was the first patient who'd refused treatment that could save his life. It's easy to calculate survival statistics. Measuring the quality of the time a person has left is harder. But your father's already in substantial pain. The surgery could make that better. If you can convince him to come back in to see me, I would really like to help him."

Cait wasn't sure what to think as she thanked the doctor and rang off. Knowing her father, she could see how much he'd hate having to learn to walk all over again with a prosthetic. And she knew better than most that once her father made up his mind about anything he wasn't likely to change it. When was the last time he'd so much as tried to see the other side of an argument?

With a sigh, she rose and went to brew a pot of tea. While the biscuits finished baking, she fried a couple of eggs over hard, the way her father liked them, and was setting marmalade on the table when she heard his cane thumping down the stairs. She closed her eyes, trying to drum up a bit of calm before she had to face him.

He came in limping heavily, his skin gray with fatigue instead of pink with sun and wind. "No need to make a fuss over breakfast," he said. "You sound like a herd of bulls clomping around in here."

"Maybe that's because your doctor just told me you need to get your strength back."

"You talked to him?"

"Yes, I did. So sit and eat what I put in front of you." Cait pulled out the chair and pointed at it sternly. "Or I'll give you a clomping the likes of which you've never seen before. That I promise you."

He stopped, his face flushing with temper. "Don't you speak to me in that tone of voice."

"If I sound like I'm speaking to a child, it's because you're behaving like one. Didn't you hear me say I've spoken with your doctor? I know exactly how selfish you're being."

"You stay out of my business."

"You don't think the fact you're deciding to kill yourself is *my* business, too? Not to mention that you couldn't be troubled to tell me you broke your leg, much less that you have cancer. And refusing treatment? That's daft even for you."

"Treatment you call it? Hah. It's butchery, plain and simple, and drugs that are more poison than medicine."

"You'd rather keep your leg and lose your life?"

"My life ended the day I put your mother in the ground," Donald snapped. "What do I have to live for?"

Cait reeled back as though he'd slapped her. Never mind how many times he'd said things like that in the past, she had never learned to expect them. Never gotten used to them. Maybe she was always going to be as thin-skinned as the child she had been when it came down to the wounds that he inflicted.

"I hoped I was worth something to you, too," she said, fighting tears away. She refused to show weakness by letting him see her cry. "This past year, I've even let myself be fooled into thinking we were becoming friends. Obviously, that was a mistake, but I am still your family. You're still my father. That's what you've told me all my life, that you were my father and that meant something. Meant that I was supposed to look up to the example that you set."

He dropped heavily into his chair, the pigheaded set of his mouth easing slightly. "This is no reflection on how much I care for you, only that I'm tired of waiting to die. Tired of being alone."

"You won't be. I'm moving home."

"I don't want you to. Your life is elsewhere, and I won't have you stuck here watching me die in slow inches while you fetch and carry for me. You already had that with your mother. Anyway, you're meant for something better than you can find around here."

"That's a shame then, isn't it? Because the

decision's made already, and before you ask me for the hundredth time what I think I'll do with myself stuck in the glen, I'll tell you. I'm going to reopen the Library and Tea Room. And if you so much as try arguing with me, I'll pour every last drop of whiskey in this house down the sink and make sure no one in the glen will sell you so much as a half a glass."

Her father's jaw went slack. "Oh, Caitie. You've quit your job? But you love it."

Since she hadn't quit yet, Cait ignored the question, tried to ignore the twist of loss that accompanied the thought of doing it. "I love the Tea Room, too," was all she said. "I love it nearly as much as I love you, so if you care for me at all, you'll fight to stay alive. I will help you fight."

"You'll nurse me and cook for me and wipe my bottom, you mean." Her father thumped the table with his fist, all the frustration and anger that had been eating at him for months coming out in his voice as he continued, "What sort of life is that?"

"The kind I'm happy to have. It's *life*. Which is what you need to be choosing. Don't you know how disappointed Mum would be to think you're willing to throw yours away? Think back to how hard she fought."

"Aye, she fought. For all the good it did her." Donald winced as he stood back up, the cane shaking as he leaned against it. "It's my decision, Cait, not yours. And it's my own right to make it. Let that be the end of the discussion. Do what you like with the Tea Room; I don't care. The money from it would have gone to you in any case, but if you want to make me happy, you'll clear out and go back to London. In fact, I don't want you in my house. Get out."

"No." Cait stuck her fists on her hips and glared at him.

He stared back at her a moment, then turned without saying another word and hobbled toward the doorway, his head high and his spine held rigid.

"Come back here and eat your breakfast," Cait called after him. "You have to eat something."

"I've lost my appetite."

"Have tea at least."

"Later," he said, hobbling toward the stairs. "I'll just go back to my room and have a wee rest in some peace and quiet first."

EMPTY SPACES

Such an empty place; so vague.
Just a country where the thunder goes
and things disappear."

TRUMAN CAPOTE
"BREAKFAST AT TIFFANY'S"

ONCE HER FATHER HAD GONE, the silence in the kitchen echoed with the things Cait should have said. But long years of living with him told her he wouldn't listen. Mrs. Bogan stropped herself along Cait's shins, complaining in Siamese.

"You've had all the breakfast you're going to get, you beggar," Cait said. But Mrs. Bogan sat in front of her, looking up so plaintively that Cait couldn't help relenting. She cut off a bit of egg and placed it on a saucer that she set down on the floor.

"May as well give it to you as see it go to waste,"

she said, then she scraped the remaining eggs into the garbage bin.

Her own appetite had fled. She salvaged the sausage and the rest of the meal, then stood helplessly, uncertain what to do. Finally, she picked up the phone.

Elspeth Murray answered straight away. "Is that you, Cait? Everything all right?"

Startled, Cait asked, "How did you know it wasn't Dad phoning?"

Elspeth sighed. "I can't remember the last time he phoned me. Told you last night, what the glen knows about your father these days comes to us through Brice, and it's a miracle Brice still has the patience for it. Looking back, it's easy to see we should have done more for Donald. Been more insistent. The old devil's always been clever with a lie, though, when it suits him. And I say that knowing full well it's the pot calling the kettle black."

"You don't know the half of the lies he's been spinning," Cait said, her voice sounding more bitter than she'd intended. "What he told Brice yesterday still wasn't close to the truth."

"What do you mean?"

"The cancer wouldn't have to be a death sentence. They can amputate the leg, and he'd have a good chance at recovery, but he's not willing to fight to live."

Elspeth was silent a long while, and when she spoke again, her tone was as brittle as the eggshells Cait had scraped into the trash. "I know that seems unthinkable to you. When you're young, with your life stretched out in front of you, death and pain are hard to understand. But sometimes, it's not about what lies ahead as much as what lies behind you. Your father said something to me one day that makes me wonder if it isn't a relief to think he can stop worrying about past mistakes. He was down at the pub with Duncan, so I didn't think much of it at the time—men tend to talk in hyperbole when they've had a few glasses too many."

"What did he say?"

"He talked about letting your mum and Robbie down. Said Robbie would still be alive if he'd only let him leave the glen instead of telling him he should stay. It's always dangerous to make assumptions like that, but it's hard to argue against the logic. Robbie was always a sweet-natured boy. Oh, he would fight to the teeth to defend someone else, the same as you, Cait, but he could never bring himself to defy your father. You were away at university, so you didn't see the way being stuck here in the glen ate at him, though. He was like a dog chewing his way out of a trap in the end. I confess, I encouraged him to leave.

Your mother did, too. He couldn't see himself withstanding your father's wrath, so in the end, he signed up for the army knowing that once he'd done that, no matter how much your father raved and ranted, there'd be no getting out of it."

Cait's fingers on the phone were numb. "Robbie loved the army," she said past a thick lump in her throat. "He was happier there than he'd ever been."

"Aye, but that doesn't change what your father thinks. To his mind, he forced Robbie to run off and get himself killed. Then your mum died, and Donald's said more than once that it was a broken heart that let the cancer take root inside her."

The small kitchen suddenly seemed even smaller, the walls closing in. Cait flung herself out the glass-topped door and turned her face into the cold, sweeping wind.

The sun had risen, washing the glen below her in a palette of winter light. The lochs reflected the freshly snow-dusted braes and the bristling white evergreens along the banks. A stag had come down the hillside for a drink, and he lifted his head as Cait watched, scenting the air before bounding away with his hooves throwing up a cloud of snow behind him.

"What can I do to help him?" she asked into the phone, sounding only half as desperate as she felt. "I have to do something."

"Out-stubborn him. Show him what he has left to live for. But you can't force him to change his mind."

"I can't compete with Robbie. I never could, and now he's dead and perfect. Forever."

"And you're alive and here. Donald was always a fool where the two of you were concerned. A fool when it came to seeing the Fletcher name live on, wanting to teach Robbie what it meant. But that doesn't mean he doesn't love you."

Cait considered that long after she'd rung off. As much as she herself had idolized Robbie—and she had—she'd resented him as well. Resented the way her father treated her as *less*. Robbie was the boy, the son, and she was the girl, an alien thing her father didn't understand and didn't always see as worth the trouble. And she *had* been trouble. Fletchers didn't run with MacLarens or get themselves excluded from school. They didn't drink or smoke or swear. Especially Fletcher girls. If her father had understood that first incident on the playground a little better, if he'd even tried to listen, Cait might have been less rebellious afterwards, but then again, maybe not. The trouble she'd gotten into had always been tangled up with loving Brice, and Brice had been plenty of trouble on his own. Some of it had been bound to rub off.

Still considering what Elspeth had said, she cleaned the kitchen until it gleamed and made a fresh cup of tea that she took upstairs for her father. He was asleep on the mattress again on the floor of the empty room, his face stamped in pain even when he wasn't conscious. Cait stood and watched him breathing a while, but she didn't have the heart to wake him. She tucked the quilt around him more tightly instead, noting how much it had picked and frayed in the time that she'd been gone, as if it had seen too much use. Mrs. Bogan crawled up beside Donald and curled herself at his feet, her crossed blue eyes half-closing almost instantly.

"That's a good girl," Cait whispered. "You stay with him even when he pretends he doesn't want you."

Then she left the barren, quiet room.

All around her, the house was a husk of what it had been. A shell vacated by its former occupants. She wondered idly whether the inside of a shell was brighter when the mollusk was still living in it and, if she'd been at her desk or had her phone with her, she would have looked that up out of curiosity. Instead, she had nothing to focus on except how much she hated the emptiness around her. Hated that her father had deliberately emptied the house of evidence that his life had once been well worth living, emptied it of color and sound and the chaos of life.

When the silence had grown too insistent, she marched herself upstairs and opened up her laptop. Trying not to let herself think of it as yet another loss, another defeat, she sent in a resignation letter which she followed with a brief phone call to her chief at the newspaper. Alice Jenkins-Pratt, whose Pulitzer Prize and brilliance had intimidated Cait more than she was willing to admit since the moment that a writing sample sent in had landed her an interview beyond her wildest expectations, was surprisingly flattering and reluctant to see Cait go.

"I wish I could tell you I could hold the position open for you," she said. "But maybe we can find you some freelance work."

"I'd like that. I'm not far from either Edinburgh or Glasgow."

"I'll think about where we can use you. You need to be hungry, though. Sniff out ideas of your own and follow your curiosity. Don't stop writing."

Cait thought of the hours her mother had always put in at the Tea Room, and how much work had gone into the library long after the doors were closed for the evening, and she suspected there'd be little chance for her to drive around chasing interviews and leads. Still, even the slim possibility of freelance work brought a surge of satisfaction that let her know just how much the job had meant to her. But she did love the Tea Room, too.

She stared at the phone after she'd hung up. That was it. She now officially had an empty calendar stretching in front of her, days and days marked with question marks.

Resolved not to let that daunt her, she scrawled a quick note and left it on the kitchen table, then she bundled herself against the cold, snatched up her keys, and let herself quietly out of the house.

What she really wanted was a start on getting rid of all that generic white at the Tea Room to burn off some of her excess energy, but it was too much to hope that Brice would have been able to find the paint this early. At his usual pace, she could expect he'd deliver *that* sometime after New Year's. Well, she'd been unfair asking him to get it for her anyway. She'd drive in to Stirling herself later, once she and her father had found time to talk a little more. In the meanwhile, the doctor had said her father needed to eat better than he had been, and since she didn't want to be out of reach too long, there was only one place to go. She could only hope that Grewer's Sweets and Groceries had someone behind the counter other than Rhona or her two vile daughters.

She had to admit, the fact that it had been Rhona of all people wearing Brice's shirt that day had made

Brice's cheating that much the more humiliating. For all that Rhona tarted herself up like a Sunday dinner and spent a fortune fighting time, she was nearly old enough to be Brice's mother.

CHALLENGE

*"No amount of fire or freshness
can challenge
what a man will store up
in his ghostly heart."*
F. SCOTT FITZGERALD
THE GREAT GATSBY

I T SCARED CAIT TO ADMIT how much she still cared what people in the glen thought about her. Anxiety bloomed in her chest as she drove down the hill and started to encounter familiar faces. Fear of acceptance was just one more thing she'd convinced herself she'd outgrown. One more instance she'd been wrong.

She'd fought so hard to get past her "wild girl" reputation when she'd come home from university after Robbie's death. She and Brice had always meant to get away once she graduated, to get away from the disapproval and the wagging tongues. She was going to work her way into a job as a journalist and Brice was going to restore cars, but after Robbie died, she hadn't had the heart. She'd come home and taken a leaf from Brando's book and clawed her way back to acceptance by volunteering for everything the village threw at her: helping with flowers at the kirk, singing in the Scottish Blend Choir, teaching art classes for the wee ones at the Village Hall, raising money to rebuild the Hall when it burned. Now, the thought of having to start all over again made her stomach ache. Once you'd had to struggle for something, it was doubly hard to lose it.

She could picture all too easily what everyone must have said about her these past months since her father had taken ill. See them leaning on their fence posts, staring up at the house with avid scowls. *Can you credit it? Cait Fletcher abandoning her poor father like this? Aye, well, what would you expect from her? Wildcats don't change their stripes.*

A small part of Cait even conceded that they wouldn't be wrong in thinking that. Had she really ever changed? It was only the things she did and the way people saw her that was different. To be honest, she'd ended up embracing the reputation they had given her as a teenager out of sheer resentment. With the pleasant warmth of too much beer, or some of Mad

Mackenzie's illegal whiskey buzzing through her bloodstream, and Brice's arm around her shoulders, it had been easier to put on a bit of swagger and ignore the disapproving, worried looks from the adults and the way the girls giggled behind her back, the way the boys nudged each other when she walked past.

That was how it was in a place that had pitted MacGregor against MacLaren for close to five hundred years. Fletchers usually sided with MacGregors against MacLarens, but after the accident that had killed Brando's parents—the accident that the village had unfairly blamed on him and Brice and the bull-tipping incident—even most of the MacLarens had taken against those two. They'd been so alone, going back to school after the funerals, trying to pretend their whole world hadn't just come crashing down. And the older boys hadn't been able to resist hurling insults. Brice, trying to protect Brando, had punched Angus McNee in the jaw and then all of Angus' mates had waded in. Eight to two hadn't seemed fair to Cait. With half the school circling around, she'd scooped up a handful of rocks and thrown them.

Luckily, only Brian Williams had been daft enough to hit a girl.

Unluckily, Cait had ended up in the Head's office

with the rest, her nose bleeding and her eye swelling, her and Brice and Brando on one side of the room while the other boys glared back from the opposite row of chairs. And that was how it had remained until the day she'd left for university. In that one unthinking moment when she was nine, she'd crossed an invisible village line that was impossible to cross back again without distancing herself from Brice.

Which was one more reason to stay as far from Brice MacLaren as she could manage now that she was back.

She rounded the bend slowly on the slippery single-track road, thinking of rebuilding relationships. When she spotted Lissa Griggs getting out of her husband's old red truck, she pulled the car to a stop. Shielding her eyes against the sunlight with a forearm, Lissa waved as she recognized Cait.

"So you're back, then? About time, too. What do you call this? Fifteen months and not so much as a single visit. Or a post card." Lissa had a coil of wire in her hand along with a pair of cutters to fix the perpetually broken fencing on the sheep pen, and some of her frizzy blond curls had, as usual, escaped the messy bun she'd scraped them into. Softening the words with a distracted smile, she moved to the fence and picked up one of a pair of fallen pickets and held it in place while waving away the cunning old black-faced ewe that was leading her contingent of sheep in yet another dash for freedom.

The familiarity of it all, the escaping sheep, the messy curls of Lissa's hair, the lightly teasing note in Lissa's voice brought a lump welling in Cait's throat.

Maybe the invisible line wasn't as impassable as she'd feared.

"He never told me," she said, "or I'd have been home like a shot."

"Aye, Brice told me yesterday. He's been telling everyone. Mind, we've all known your father's a daft old devil, but we'd never have thought this of him. Looking back, I'm ashamed of myself for not doing more for him."

"What do you mean?" Cait asked.

"Been making a proper hermit of himself, hasn't he? Whole time since you've been gone. Scarcely leaves the cottage and won't answer the door when someone stops by with a pudding or a bit of stew. That only got worse when he broke his leg. Weren't for Brice, we'd have had to ring you ages ago."

You should have rung me anyway. Someone could have rung me, Cait thought, but "Thank you for trying to help," was all she said.

Lissa rubbed at her sleeve, dislodging the dusting of snow that had fallen from the larch tree at the edge of the road. "Should have tried harder," she said, looping wire around the fencepost. "But you know how folks can be. Some—and I won't say who—were putting it about that you'd gotten above yourself with your grand London job, but I never believed it. The way things used to be between you and your father before Robbie died, it made more sense to think the two of you had fallen out again." She smiled a bit too brightly. "But there. It's all water under the bridge now, isn't it? You're home, and I've no doubt you'll soon see things right."

Cait wished she had Lissa's confidence as they said their goodbyes. Leaving Lissa to fix the fence before the sheep could make a more determined sprint for liberty, she proceeded downhill at a cautious pace. The sharp curve after the turn-off to Brice's cottage and the garage where he'd worked since long before his father died had always iced over early and melted late. She slowed even more as she approached it.

Good thing, too. Brice's car barreled toward her coming up from town, and he took the shoulder so that they scraped by each other in the curve with a whisker's width of air between them. He had the nerve to grin and wave, and Cait watched the glossy Land Rover rush out of sight in her rearview mirror. Then she shook her head and told herself sternly to pay attention to the road.

Still, she couldn't help wondering where he'd been. There was only one reason he would be up this early and heading home, and it struck Cait like a kick to the stomach. She wasn't sure she could bear it if she had to watch someone else standing beside him at the tree lighting, see him kissing someone else beneath the traditional ball of mistletoe they'd be bringing down to the village. Tonight, she realized belatedly. The lighting was tonight, and she couldn't decide whether it would be better to go and face everyone, start the process of redeeming herself all over again straight away, or take the coward's route and hide at home.

It would all depend on her father, though, wouldn't it? She could hardly leave him on his own when she'd only just gotten back.

Mindful that she might need to work even harder to gain acceptance if she *wasn't* at the tree lighting, she was even more careful to stop and greet everyone she met on the road. Near the old oak tree that had been split by lightening the night before her sixteenth birthday, she chatted briefly with Angus Greer and his heavily-pregnant Kirsty outside their cottage. Kirsty had worked at the Tea Room for years, and they were on the MacGregor side of things anyway, so they were friendly. Brice's second cousin Rory, though, who she ran into a moment later, fell straight back into flirting with her as if she'd never been gone, as if she'd never left Brice practically at the altar. Only old Mrs. Ewing refused to so much as acknowledge her, standing in her front window holding Samson, the little Wheaten terrier who had only half as much propensity to bite as his owner. Cait told herself Mrs. Ewing had always been a right old witch anyway and it didn't matter, but she was still feeling the chill of the encounter as she got out of the car in front of Grewer's Sweets and Groceries a few moments later.

Expecting the usual off-white rows of display shelves crammed with tinned beans and laundry soap, she stopped inside the doorway and blinked in surprise at the wooden screens painted with views of the glen at its most beautiful that now divided the rest of the shop from a row of charmingly mismatched cafe-style tables draped in a variety of tartan plaids. Moving past those, she saw that the old refrigerated case that had previously displayed Rhona's daily offering of baked goods had gained a twin. And where the variety of pies and cakes and scones had always been uninspired, there was now an eye-popping selection of exquisitely-decorated miniature Scottish tarts as well as French-style mille-feuilles, tartes tatin, and macarons. Atop the display case, a three-tier serving stand positioned beside a cute polka-dotted teapot held a sampling of delicate sandwiches and a selection of pastries with a hand-lettered sign:

CREAM TEAS OFFERED

1:00-5:00 PM

FROM £10.50

Cait's rage meter rose instantly from low to sizzling.

Rhona Grewer had wasted no time at all taking advantage of the Tea Room closing.

As if what Rhona had done before hadn't been enough already.

The bells on the door behind Cait had scarcely stopped jingling when Rhona herself swept in through the curtain of beads that concealed the stock room. As brassy blond and tarted up as ever, she wore zebra-striped stiletto heels and another of her tight pencil skirts, but her slithery satin blouse was partially covered by a pink and brown polka-dotted apron that matched the teapot on the display case. Her smile widened into a crocodile's grin as she caught sight of Cait.

"Oh," she said. "You're back, are you? I'd heard you preferred to stay in London."

"You heard? Or you've been telling people so?" Cait countered.

Rhona shrugged rather viciously. "I can't help

what people might overhear, now can I? Did you come in to shop or were you looking for Brice? If so, you've only just missed him."

Cait willed her face to show no emotion. "I stopped in for food, actually. You do still sell groceries, I assume?"

"If you're referring to the fact I'm serving teas," Rhona said, blushing, "that's business, plain and simple. Your father closed the Tea Room, and someone needs to offer the tourists a place to grab a bite. Not everyone can afford to eat at the hotel. But it's worked beautifully for me, I have to say." She straightened the sign on the counter and turned the teapot a fraction of an inch clockwise as if that somehow made a difference. "Brando gives me a lovely discount on the pastries, and all I have to do is make the sandwiches, which is far less work than when I was doing all the baking on my own. Shame your father didn't think of that. He might have found a way to keep the Tea Room open, but you can't blame me for that. I'd have been mad to pass up the opportunity when I saw it."

"I can't think when you last passed up an opportunity to stir up trouble," Cait responded mildly.

Clearly, she was going to need to have a chat with Brando.

Not that she meant to take away *his* business. If

he was offering Rhona a wholesale discount, it might mean that the hotel and his bakery down in Callander were struggling, too. Asking him not to sell to Rhona would put him in a tough position, so Cait would need to think of an alternative.

Overall, she had a lot of thinking to do.

Turning from Rhona with a muffled sigh, she snatched up a basket from a stack strategically positioned beside one of the pastry cases where everyone buying groceries would be forced to get an eyeful of tempting sweets. That was another problem with Rhona—in addition to being a conniving witch fully capable of flirting at Olympic level, she was too bloody clever by half.

Well, two could play at that.

Cait had no intention of letting Rhona steal the Tea Room's customers. Rhona'd already stolen more than Cait could ever forgive, and the Tea Room held too many important memories, not only for Cait but for everyone in the glen. That couldn't be replaced by six tables in the front window of a glorified mini-market.

The Tea Room's legacy had to be preserved, and thanks to Rhona, Cait would have to find a way to not only reopen quickly, but also to bring the customers in.

MISTAKES

"Everything tells me that
I am about to
make a wrong decision,
but making mistakes
is just part of life."

PAOLO COELHO
ELEVEN MINUTES

A FTER BANGING THROUGH THE KITCHEN DOOR
with her arms laden, Cait opened the refrigerator
to put the groceries away and discovered that someone
stocked it up already. A fresh quart of milk that hadn't
been there earlier stood on the rack along with a
packet of chicken breasts, a head of lettuce, tomatoes,
and a bottle of orange juice. And on the table,
someone had filled a vase with a bouquet of pine and
holly sprigs and placed it beside a plate of disturbingly

familiar-looking pastries.

There was no sign of a note.

Cait emptied the two reusable shopping bags of groceries, picked up Mrs. Bogan, and absently scratched the cat behind the ears as she headed into the sitting room in search of her father. He wasn't there, but when she went upstairs and listened at his door, she thought she heard him moving around. She gave a cautious knock.

"What?" he barked. "I'm sleeping."

Nothing wrong with the old man's hearing, then.

"You're not sleeping or you wouldn't be talking," she said.

"Who can sleep with you banging around?"

She tested the knob and poked her head in the door when she found it wasn't locked. "I only just got back from the shop," she said, "but someone had come by and left groceries in the kitchen. Any idea who that might have been?"

"That Brice. He's got the key." Her father sat on the edge of the lonely mattress with his pale, scrawny legs splayed out in front of him while he struggled to pull trousers on over his pajama bottoms.

Cait pretended not to notice either the state of him or the emptiness of the room. She merely raised an eyebrow. "You gave Brice the key to the house?"

Her father's cheeks turned red. Ducking his head,

he reached for the cane that lay on the floor nearby. "Why shouldn't I?"

"Because you never had a kind word to say to him in all the time he and I went out together. I can't help thinking it's suspicious you're finding him useful now that we've broken up."

"I never said he was useful. Only less use*less* than the rest around here." Donald used the cane to lever himself upright, and it shook only marginally less than his legs and spindly arms.

Cait had to keep herself from rushing across the floor to help him. He wouldn't have thanked her for it. The back of her eyes felt heavy and hot with tears, and she had to swallow them down, clearing her throat before she spoke again.

"I don't begin to understand you," she said, then she shook her head. "I'll go make some tea for you. You're going to eat something now if I have to push it down you, you stubborn old bull."

"Listen to how you're talking to your father, now." Donald's face went even redder. "You can just get out of this house if this is how you're going to be. I forgot what a mule-headed brat you always were."

Cait's hands flew to her hips. "And who do you think I got that from? I'm going nowhere, Dad, I'll tell you that much. Neither are you if I have anything to say about it."

He leaned his large frame heavily on the cane. "Good thing you haven't, then," he said, "because I'm dying. Now get out so I can finish dressing."

Cait stared at him squint-eyed, her mouth so full of words she couldn't say a single one. Finally, she whipped around and stalked back downstairs to the kitchen where she slammed the kettle on the stove and banged the lid of the teapot on the counter hard enough to break a chip off of it.

What was she going to do? How was she supposed to convince him that he had to fight?

He was hurting, and she couldn't begin to reach that kind of pain.

The fact that she was hurting herself made her want to run to Brice and have him hold her, have him listen. Old habits, old loves, old hurts, died hard.

Thinking on that made it easier to understand how hopeless, how alone, her father must feel without her mother. As often as Cait had wondered how her mother could possibly put up with his demands, his petty tyranny, his need to give his opinion on everything and everyone while always insisting that *he* was always right, she had never doubted the love between them.

Now when she reflected on it, it struck her that love had to be the greatest miracle of all the many miracles that made up the world in which they lived. The simple knowledge that the most difficult people to love could be loved as much, as hard, as deeply, as anyone else offered the promise of redemption.

She made her father's breakfast for the second time that morning and, once she'd seen him settled on the sofa in front of the telly, she drove back to the Tea Room to check the cellar. Surely there had to be leftover paint there in a forgotten corner—something other than the stark, empty white that Brice had been using. She felt desperate to burn off some energy, and temper, and she always thought best when her hands were busy.

But as she drove into the car park, she discovered that Brice's Land Rover was already there. She stopped her own car beside it, turned off the ignition, tried to talk herself into the courage to go inside while the cold slowly seeped in around her and her breath fogged the windows.

The Brice that had filled a vase with pine and holly was a Brice she didn't know. And wherever he'd spent the night, he'd bought food at the shop and driven it up to the house first thing, thinking to save her a trip. He had always been many things, many lovely things, but that particular kind of thoughtfulness had never been among them.

He'd told her he was changing. Maybe he'd been right.

She eased herself out of the car and paused beside it, holding the top of the driver's door, trying to decide what she would say to him. A part of her—the stormy, unruly part she'd been working to keep tightly leashed—craved the emotional release of a good fight, the kind she and Brice had always done so well. The kind that ended in making up and laughter. They'd been good at that, too, but that wasn't an option now.

"Thank you for taking care of my father," she said simply, honestly, when she found him inside sanding a plank he'd put up across two sawhorses in the leftmost of the cozy seating areas that served as quiet reading nooks.

He straightened and stood holding the electric sander in one hand, the sleeves of his sweater pushed up on wiry forearms, and his stubborn jaw softened as she finished speaking.

"You're welcome," he said, his voice softer, too.

With a small shiver, Cait remembered that voice, that very one, whispering in her ear. Whispering that he loved her. Needed her. Whispering that she was the most beautiful woman he'd ever seen.

The memories squeezed her heart and wrung it dry, leaving regret rattling like autumn leaves inside her chest. Regret was bitter and smelt of loss, and she was sick of loss, of all the cold, empty emotions. It was something bright and sweet and heady that she needed. Hope. Comfort. Courage.

She strode across the room and placed her hands flat against Brice's cheeks, pulling his mouth down to hers, meeting him on her toes.

He froze in place a moment. Then the electric sander thudded on the floor and his arms came around her, moved up her back, pulled her close, closer, and closer still. He lifted her until her legs wrapped around him of their own accord, and he sat her on the top of the board that he'd been sanding and kissed her while the fire that had always been between them, the fire that she had tried to convince herself had died, flashed back into blue-hot flame and proved that it had been banked instead of snuffed.

Who had she been fooling? Of all the people in the world, Brice had the capacity to hurt her more than anyone precisely because she loved him more than she'd ever thought it was possible to love another human being. Because he was a part of her.

She kissed him, answered his kisses, while the sun shone like a gem on the snow outside the window, and as much as she had loved her work in London, she suspected she hadn't felt this alive since the moment she had left the glen. Since the moment when she'd last kissed Brice.

Breaking away, she drew back. "You broke my heart," she whispered. "You're probably going to break it again."

"You're a fine one to talk," he said. "Do you know how I felt when I found your note? When you returned your ring and wouldn't take my calls?"

"You had Rhona," Cait said, sounding as bitter as she felt.

"I never had anyone except you, Cait. Not since my mother left. I had you and Brando, and you're all I've ever needed or wanted. I had a drink with Rhona—a few drinks, aye. But that was all. I didn't stop to think—"

"You never do. You don't consider. You leap. Headlong. Och, you mean well—we all know that. You're not malicious. You're a good man, Brice, but your thoughtlessness hurts the people around you. You don't stop to realize that just one moment of being impulsive, taking people up on what they offer, not saying stop soon enough, that one moment is all it takes."

"Don't you think I know that?" He drew back, stood looking at the wall above her head. The muscles tightened in his cheeks. "You're not the only one who got hurt. I had to live without you once you'd gone. I had to stay here after you left, while Davy Grigg took bets from everyone in the entire glen about what exactly I'd done to send you flying out of here like that. It never occurred to a single one of them that you were the one who needed to leave."

"I didn't."

"Aye, you did. It took the both of us to make a mistake that big."

"*Was* it a mistake? Truly?" Cait asked, watching him, wanting him to deny it. Wanting, deep down, for him to say something to make it—make them—all right again.

He searched her expression and found her vulnerability. Cait's every nerve ending tingled, anticipating him reaching for her. Hoping he would.

Because this time, if he did, it wouldn't be recklessness or impulse that brought them together again. He was thinking about it. She was thinking.

Only he didn't reach for her. He backed away another step instead and picked the sander up from the floor. "No," he said. "It wasn't a mistake. Not entirely. We both needed the time away. We both needed to grow up."

AMBITION

S TEPPING AWAY FROM CAIT at that moment was one of the hardest things Brice had ever done, but the physical side of their relationship had never been the problem. He needed her to see that he *had* changed. He needed her to see him differently. And he needed to know that she had grown past their adolescent baggage, too. *She* needed to know that she had grown into herself.

He stepped back and watched her pride wrestle with doubt, with rejection. He regretted that. She jumped down from her perch on the shelf that he'd been sanding, and in typical Cait fashion, she burned off energy pacing as she changed the subject. But as she told him what the doctor had said about her father, his attention refocused. When he held her again, it was about comfort, about sharing pain. He would have taken all of it from her if he could have. He wished there was a way to do that—Cait had lived through too much pain already.

"So you've apparently been taking care of him when no one else in the village would—"

"They would have, if he'd let them," Brice corrected.

"Fine. But now how do I convince him to have the surgery? I can't accept that he's just throwing the rest of his life away."

"You can't force him to want to live." Brice stroked the familiar silk of her hair. "All you can do is love him enough to let him have dignity in the choice he makes."

She rested her cheek against his chest. "I'd like to slap sense into his stubborn head."

Brice couldn't help laughing at that. "You tend to want to do that a lot."

"Only when someone deserves it."

"Only when *you* think someone deserves it." He hadn't planned on denying it anymore—she had to trust him or a relationship between them was worthless anyway—but he couldn't help himself. He needed her to know. "I never slept with Rhona," he said. "I know what you think you saw, but she only came to see what I could do with the car. I made the mistake of drinking with her when I told her it was beyond saving. She'd brought the bottle because she was afraid of that and wanted to say goodbye—"

"She'd have brought it to celebrate if you'd told her you could save it."

"Probably, but I wasn't thinking. She raised a glass to the car, and then to me trying to save it, then to me helping her find a new one because she'd only just bought that one a few months back. One toast slid into another, and then she noticed she'd gotten grease on her blouse and insisted on washing it out before it set. The shirt you'd given me was hanging on the back of the chair in my bedroom, and she came out wearing it, and while she'd been gone I realized I'd had too much to drink so I told her to leave and I went in to sober up in the shower the second I'd closed the door behind her. That's all that happened. So maybe you're right about me not thinking when I take people up on what they offer. I was stupid to drink with her—I don't drink to get drunk these days. Not anymore. That's one of the things I've learned."

"One of the things?" Cait asked, watching him. Her face gave nothing away.

"The rest I'll have to show you back at the garage if you're willing to consider staying."

"Oh, I'm staying. For my father's sake."

"That wasn't what I meant." He brushed her hair back from her face and rubbed the pads of his thumbs across her temples. "I haven't stopped loving you. I couldn't. You're as much a part of me as my memories, as every dream I ever had, as the fingers on my hands. But what we had together, the old relationship, that had to change because we aren't children anymore. We can't love the way children do. Will you let me court you now, *mo leannan*? Court you properly? Let me give you time to get to know me, to know the two of us as we are right now?"

Her breath hitched, then brushed against his skin as she let it all out in one deep exhale. "I'd like that," she said, "but my father—"

"If your father needs anything to make him want to live, it's to see life going on around him. The last thing you want to do is hang around the house waiting on him hand and foot. That will only make the both of you want to hurry the end along."

"That's an awful thing to say," Cait said, but she couldn't help laughing.

Brice had missed the sound of her laughter more than anything.

It made him want to spend a lifetime making her

laugh.

Letting her go, he went back to the shelf and ran his hand across the edge of it, feeling for any rough spots that still needed to be smoothed away. "You know why Donald didn't tell you he was sick, don't you?" he asked. "Why he told you to stay in London?"

"Elspeth claims it's because he feels guilty about Robbie dying."

"He feels like he stole Robbie's life as well as your mum's. Like the glen stole away the lives those two could have had and forced them to settle for something smaller. It's why he's determined you won't end up stuck here. With me. Why he doesn't want you taking up with me again."

"You know an awful lot about him these days." Cait came to stand beside Brice again and slanted a look up at him.

"He needed someone—and I don't mean anything by that. Nothing against you. I'm just saying that, for a time, he needed someone who wouldn't challenge him, who would listen and do what needed to be done."

"So you became Robbie for him?"

"I became whatever he needed me to be, aye, but the reason he allowed it was because he doesn't care what I think of him. He only cares about the people he respects."

"Then why do it? Why help him?"

He was looking down at the board, and Cait suddenly reached down and put her hand on his to keep it still. He felt the warmth of her skin, the softness of it. It was so small and pale compared to his calloused, sun-browned paws.

Turning his palm over, he caught her fingers in his own and brought them to his lips. "For your sake," he said. "I suppose it started with me wanting to earn his acceptance. A step toward winning you back. That was the first part of realizing I wanted to change myself for you. Then I discovered I wanted to change for my own sake. Somewhere along the way, I went from nearly hating Donald to feeling sorry for him to liking him more than I'd expected."

"He's never been particularly likable," Cait said. "Even Mum admitted that."

Brice pulled her closer. "You remember Haggis, don't you?" he asked, thinking of the old black and white mongrel who had so often been the only company he'd had in the house as he grew up. "He died this year while you were gone. I used to get angry when people couldn't see that, no matter how much he snarled and barked, all he wanted to do was be your friend. He just didn't know how to go about it. Not everyone is brave enough to show that they're afraid."

She paused and studied him, a look on her face that made him feel, for once, as though he'd done something right. But then, Cait had always made him feel like that.

Even when he'd done nothing right at all.

"I'm sorry about Haggis," she said, her voice thick with tears. "I know how much you loved him." Squeezing her eyes shut suddenly, she folded her hands across the back of her head and tilted up her chin. "God, we're a mess, aren't we? All of us. So much loss, and I'm sorry about so many things. I don't know what I believe about Dad feeling guilty over Robbie. I'm going to have to spend time thinking about that. Maybe there's no right answer. The army never was part of Robbie's original plan, that much is true. All he wanted to do was travel, see the places Mum talked about: Greece, Italy, America. But once he was in the army, he loved it. Loved having mates, being part of a unit, something bigger. He gave his life to save his friends from dying. I think he'd have said he was happy to die that way, that he was happy his death had meaning. He probably wouldn't have been there if it weren't for Dad, but I don't know that he'd consider that a bad thing. And Mum? She may have had other dreams originally, but she loved the glen and her life here. I hate that Dad feels she wasted herself.

He's diminishing her by thinking that."

Brice had forgotten how much he loved the way Cait's mind worked, the passion and the fairness and the fierce, determined loyalty of it.

"So show your father that he's wrong," he said.

Cait blinked. Refocused. "How do I do that?"

He blew a bit of dust off the curved edge of the board and rubbed his palms together to brush them off. "That's what you'll need to figure out. But you know him. Telling him what to do won't do a bloody bit of good. You'll have to find a way to make him see it for himself."

Cait shook her head and stared hard at the floor, thinking. "None of this is what I was expecting to find when I got here. None of it," she said. "Which reminds me. Do you happen to know what he did with all Mum's things?"

"From the house, you mean? I stowed them away in the attic. He couldn't bear to see them, but I knew you'd hate it if he sold them or put them in the bin."

"Thank you. For that and everything else. For helping here." She turned away as if she couldn't bear to have him see the moisture that had crept into her eyes. After a moment, she walked over to the two shelves he'd already mounted on the wall behind her and, making a show of examining them, she ran her fingers along the beveled edges. "I know you have other things to do besides putting up bookshelves. Elspeth told me you've been busy. But I'll need to reopen as soon as I can now that Rhona's started serving teas. I don't want her efforts hitting the online review sites and getting listed anywhere while the Tea Room drops out of sight. Anyway, it feels disloyal to Mum, somehow, letting the teas for the glen be served in Rhona's market."

"Not to mention it would drive you crazy," he said, knowing her too well to let that slide. "But you know she isn't likely to let that go anytime soon. Not now that she's spent money on the tables and the screens. Her shop's on the main road, too, in easy sight of the graveyard, which gives her better traffic."

"I'm trying to think of a way to get the tourists here, don't you worry about that. I'll make up claims as wild as Elspeth's if I have to."

Brice laughed, picturing the Tea Room full of illustrated signs with made up history like the ones Elspeth had in her museum. "I can see it now. You could put a sign on every table: 'Rob Roy MacGregor ate here' or 'Robert the Bruce sat here and drank a cuppa.' But go ahead. If the tourists want to believe Elspeth's got Bonnie Prince Charlie's dagger on display in the back room at Breagh House, they'll eat up just about any story you want to tell them."

"I don't have to tell them made up stories, though, do I?" Cait's face had taken on an odd, thoughtful expression.

A dangerous expression.

"What are you up to now, Cait Fletcher?"

Cait's schemes had often been far wilder than any good-natured lies Elspeth Murray spun about odd bits of Highland history to go with her so-called "artifacts."

"Why would I need made-up stories about Rob Roy MacGregor or Robert the Bruce when I've got something better and absolutely real. I've got Mum's Scottish shortbread recipe that came down in her family from Mary Queen of Scots, if I can find it. The tourists love stories about Mary, don't they? Anyway, there's more than enough places in the Highlands dedicated to glorifying men in kilts. I'll make the Library and Tea Room a monument to Scottish women. It's about time someone remembered who it was did the real hard work while the men were off raiding cattle or playing war."

Brice might have pointed out, gently, that there was no such thing as "playing war," but when Cait had that look in her eye, there was no sense in arguing with her. Anyway, once he thought on it, was she really that far off the mark? Not the first time a boy marched off to battle anyway. If he survived the first battle, he wasn't a boy any longer, and war stopped being a game of any kind, stopped being about ideas or lines on a map for the survivors. It became all too personal, then, about brothers like her Robbie and friends and loved ones lost.

"Make it personal, then," he said. "Not only about the famous women the tourists know already, the Mary MacGregors and Flora MacDonalds and Mary Stewarts. Make it about women like your mum and Elspeth and the others in the glen."

A deep rose color unfurled like a banner across Cait's cheekbones, the way it did when she'd caught hold of an idea that warmed her from the inside out. That was another thing Brice had missed about her. In another life, Cait Fletcher would have been a Flora or a Mary, a woman who changed the course of history. And watching her take fire as she was thinking, he could understand why Donald wanted her out of the glen, wanted her to reach for something bigger than she'd find in a tiny village in a tiny glen. Brice had planned to go with her once. He still would. He'd follow her anywhere, if that was the only choice left to him. But these days, whenever he imagined the two of them growing old together, they were always here, in the house he'd been building for Cait this past year in the hope that she'd come home to him. He could see the two of them sitting there on the porch together, looking out across the lochs toward the high, steep Munros that guarded the far end of the narrow glen.

Was it selfish to hope that life here, with him, could be enough for her? That he could be enough?

BATTLES

*"A love for tradition has never
weakened a nation,
indeed it has strengthened nations
in their hour of peril."*

WINSTON S. CHURCHILL

T HEY WORKED TOGETHER, DISCUSSING POSSIBILITIES, for about an hour before Brice excused himself, pleading something about a car he had to finish. Cait stood beside the window with her arms wrapped around herself, cold and a little lonely as she watched his Land Rover pull away. Only now that he was gone did she allow herself to reflect on the sharp stab of rejection that had pierced her chest when he'd pulled away from her—and the relief when he'd explained.

Neither of which were emotions she could—

should—allow herself.

Was he right, though? Was there some other way forward in their relationship? Something beyond the rocky single-mindedness of adolescent love? Or maybe all first loves were single-minded. Self-indulgent. Looking back, she could see how they'd been wrapped up in the *idea* of loving each other almost as much as they'd been entangled in the feelings.

Brice had changed, she had to give him that. Far more than she had changed. The Brice she had known would never have left a vase of greens, not without a note that expected credit. He wouldn't have put up with her father all these months without exploding. Most of all, he wouldn't have advocated caution.

Neither of them had ever advocated caution.

She turned from the window and looked around the room. Brice had mounted six shelves on the bare white wall before he left, the unstained wood contributing to the emptiness of the place now that he was gone. Funny how he had filled it up. But eyeing the effect of the shelves, she had to admit that they were much nicer than the heavy dark oak bookcases had been. Even the white paint might not be entirely bad once the books were back in place, letting the walls recede in a way that the old burgundy and hunter green walls never had. What the place needed was something in between. Wallpaper, maybe. Something Victorian and charming. Or no. Going back to the idea of honoring the women of the glen, each of the rooms should have a different Highland theme, one room in tartan plaid with tartan curtains and tartan ribbon edging around the bookshelves, and another in the soft purple hues of Highland heather stenciled on the walls. She'd hang dozens of old photos and prints of women, some famous, but most of them just the everyday, ordinary heroes who fed and clothed their men and bairns, kept the homes, and raised future generations to hope for better than they had themselves, all while achieving small miracles in their communities without asking for accolades or rewards.

This room, Cait's old favorite, she would dedicate to her mother. And she would dedicate the main seating area to all the women of the glen together. She only needed to find the photographs, and she knew just where to get them.

She stopped by Elspeth Murray's before going home, because Elspeth was better at spreading news than a BBC emergency alert. And Elspeth pulled the front door open the moment that Cait rang the bell at Breagh House, almost as if Cait had been expected.

"Well, you look happier than you did the last time I saw you, I must say," Elspeth announced, stepping back to let Cait in.

Cait grinned, acknowledging to herself that for the first time since she'd arrived, maybe for the first time since her mother's death, she felt something that was beginning to resemble—not joy, not that. Hope, anticipation. A sense that she was in the right place, taking the right steps forward.

"I need your help," she said, and over a pot of tea and a plate of Elspeth's biscuits, she explained, then explained all over again once Elspeth had called a handful of other women and invited them over.

They drank tea and ate and debated—because nothing happened in the village without debate—which of the women in their own families deserved to be honored. It was a weighty decision, after all, because it wouldn't do to include someone and slight someone else. And what exactly was a hero, anyway?

"Well, we can all agree on Mary MacGregor. And Connal's grandmother. There's the distillery, too," Flora Macara said, then she sprinted out of her chair and out through the back door as Shame, the Inn's unruly golden retriever, gave a deep *halloooo* of a bark and set off in pursuit of a silver Audi that was driving toward Inverlochlarig House down at the far end of the road. "Oy," Flora shouted. "Shame, you get back here and leave those poor folks alone."

Shame glanced back at her over his shoulder, ran

a few steps, and then evidently decided that he wasn't likely to catch the vehicle anyway. At least that was Cait's suspicion, because the dog had never been known to listen to a thing either Flora or her husband Duncan said.

Cheeks bright with the cold, Flora unlooped the battered brown leather belt that was holding up her mud-colored skirt, threaded it through Shame's collar, and stood looking around the yard behind the kitchen. "You have a bit of rope here anywhere, Elspeth?" she asked. "The idiot dog won't go away until I do, so I'll need to tie him up."

"You'd better bring him inside here, then. Where it's warm," Elspeth told her, pushing the kitchen door open wider and standing back as the four other women crowded in the doorway retreated, too.

Flora, her big-boned, almost masculine face redeemed by blue eyes that were generally as shrewd as they were lovely, marched Shame back inside and winced at the filthy prints he left all across Elspeth's kitchen floor. Spotting Cait, the dog bounded toward her, wrenching himself out of Flora's grasp. Cait only laughed as he stood on his hind legs, muddy paws nearly at her shoulders while he did his best to lick her face.

"Shame! Get down. Bad dog!" Flora shouted.

"I'm sorry, love," she said to Cait. "You know how he's always escaping."

Cait thought of Robbie, and the sheep, even herself. Her father. Going all the way back as far as Rob Roy MacGregor trying to escape the Duke of Montrose. Someone in the glen was always trying to escape.

She shook her head and instructed Shame to sit, which he did with perfect amiability, his plume of a tail sweeping the floor behind him.

"What were you saying about the distillery?" she asked when things had calmed again and they'd all sat back down at the table with their teacups.

"You've heard that story, surely?" Flora insisted. "It's your own family history, lass. Before the distillery closed, it was. Back in the world wars when most of the men in the glen had gone off to fight, your great grandmother organized the women of the glen to step in and distill the whiskey, navigating all the new wartime restrictions. They transported it, too, and found new distribution. Wasn't until the end of World War II that they realized so many of the men had died there wasn't any sense trying to keep the jobs open anymore. Time of the Great War, we Scots made up ten percent of Britain's population, but our men made up thirteen percent of the volunteers who fought. That took a toll between the wars, then come the second war, it wasn't only the fighting that cost us. Those who didn't march off to battle went down to Glasgow and Edinburgh to work in the factories and shipyards. And the women, meanwhile, kept the glen running same as they'd always done. Things don't change so much. A regiment of 'kilties' marching to the pipes still strikes the fear of God into an enemy, but it's the women back home who let the men go off and be heroic."

Cait studied the faces of the women around her, none of them particularly glamorous, but each one beautifully marked by hard years of living. Excepting only herself, everyone around the table was old enough to remember fathers and grandfathers and brothers lost in wartime, and in the rebuilding that came after. They'd seen children and loved ones move away in search of opportunity and watched the tourists sweep in to transform the Highlands, the way tourists were bringing chaos and change to so many of the other peaceful places in the world.

Cait hadn't planned to go to the tree lighting in the village that night. There hadn't seemed to be much worth celebrating, and the whole idea of facing the village, facing Brice, had seemed too awkward. But as the women around her spoke with excitement in their voices about the old photographs they had at home and wanted to show her, and talked about the memories Cait's project was stirring up, she remembered tree lightings with her mother and father holding hands and kissing beneath the mistletoe. She remembered carrying her first candle when she was five and Robbie lifting her so that she could clip it to the tree. Robbie had lowered her down afterwards. Then he'd tugged his wool cap onto her head because she'd stubbornly refused to wear her own hat when they'd left the house and her father had told her she could bloody well freeze, if so.

She remembered Brice wiping the cold tears from her cheeks as she lit her candle in remembrance of Robbie the year he died.

She had told herself, while she was away in London, that there had been too much emphasis on tradition in the glen. At Christmas and Hogmanay and Beltane and Easter Sunday, this past year, at each of the occasions that the village enthusiastically marked with some leftover ceremony whose origin no one remembered, she had told herself that she was happy to miss the fuss. But traditions were important, she realized. The things and memories that families shared, mothers passed down to daughters, and fathers passed down to sons. Too many of the young people from the glen were gone, dead like Robbie or moved away. The old folks too often had no one with whom to share the memories of their lives.

Seeing how happy these women were to share their stories with her, it occurred to her that change itself was the modern battle, and from that there might be no escape. Maybe the glen was right to embrace as much tradition as it could.

The seeds of the idea that had begun with the photographs began to expand inside her, along with a building sense of excitement. Because it wasn't the photographs that she would hang on the walls that ultimately mattered. The lives behind the photographs were more important, and the women—who they had been, what they had done, and what they'd passed down to their children.

Just this morning, Cait had felt regret for the career that she had started to build for herself in London. Now, she wondered if losing those fledgling dreams hadn't simply opened up opportunities she hadn't dreamed of yet. Whatever happened with her father, whatever happened with Brice, maybe she had a life here to carve out for herself. She didn't know exactly how the stories and photographs connected yet, but instinct told her they would be important, not only to the Tea Room, but to her as well, and maybe to the entire glen.

ESCAPING

*"Think you're escaping
and run into yourself.
Longest way round
is the shortest way home."*

JAMES JOYCE
ULYSSES

T he television needed to be smashed. Cait sent it a sour look.

"You're wasting away," she said to her father, "and I won't have it. Now stop staring mindlessly at the telly and eat this soup I made you."

Her father mashed the television remote with his thumb, increasing the volume repeatedly to drown her out. Cait set the bowl on the coffee table, her hand shaking enough to slosh out a floating bit of carrot and a good spoonful or two of chicken broth to which she'd added a few pieces of mashed potato, giving extra substance to the old standby Cock-a-leekie recipe she'd made with her mother a hundred times. Maybe she should have realized her father wouldn't want to eat anything that reminded him of Mum, but what was Cait supposed to feed him? Frozen dinners?

She strode around behind the television set and pulled the plug out of the wall. "Now you listen to me, old man. I'm not going to let you starve yourself to death any more than I'm going to let you die any other way. You had enough energy to lie to me, and that's more than enough to eat a spoonful or two of soup."

"You can go back to London anytime you like." He glared and rolled over, turning his back on her.

She went and sat at his shoulder. "I'm right where I want to be," she said. "I love you."

"I never said I don't love you." Her father sat up, painfully slow, and his voice was gruff, as if the words themselves were painful. But then, Cait didn't remember ever having heard him say them. Not to her, nor Robbie for that matter. Not even to her mother. He looked away. "What's the point of making me draw all this out?" he asked. "It'll only ruin what you remember of me in the end."

"Or give me something new that's worth remembering. You want to tell me this is how Donald Fletcher wants to be remembered? As the man who

140

didn't have an ounce of fight left in him? A man who ran from the battle and watched the telly instead of fighting?"

"What good would I be with half a leg? You don't understand. You've never been useless." The blue of his eyes had faded, too, somehow, the spit and fire within them dying down.

"I've felt useless most of my life," Cait said, knowing he'd made her feel that way. But she finally let that go. Gently, she took his hand. "But if having the leg amputated is the problem, then explain why you think it's too hard. Show me you've thought it through. They have great prosthetics these days, and you're the one who taught us that Fletchers never quit."

"Wish I never had taught you that. You might have given up on Brice MacLaren years ago, and you wouldn't be here nagging at me now."

"Brice has nothing to do with this conversation, and he's been good to you while I've been gone. You can't deny that."

"That's because he has a guilty conscience, knowing he drove you away and made you leave." Tipping his head, Donald pulled his hand away and folded his arms across his thin chest, daring Cait to contradict him.

141

Since he'd opened the door, she decided to sail straight through it however cruel it might seem. Arguing had always energized her father, lent him fuel.

"It seems to me," she said, "the guilty conscience belongs to you. You think you drove Robbie away, but you didn't. He wanted to go, and he died with honor, doing what he loved. I hate the fact that he's gone as much as you do, but I won't let you diminish his life by making his death about you instead of about his bravery. If you want to feel guilty, feel guilty about what you've done to Brice. Using him the way you have."

"He offered—"

"Aye, but did you ever give him a word of thanks?"

"I must have done."

"There you go, revising history again. Also, you know full well you're the one who talked me into leaving that day I came home storming mad. You went and got the suitcase for me and told me not to stay or I'd end up embarrassing myself by forgiving him. That I'd only be giving him permission to cheat on me over and over again if I didn't leave."

Her father looked back at her across his shoulder. "What's so wrong about that? You're a Fletcher, girl. You don't stay with any man who doesn't want you."

"Weren't you the one who taught me that anything worth having is worth fighting for?"

Her father stared at her and she stared back, reluctant to give ground. Then Mrs. Bogan chose that moment to put her front paws on the sofa and peer up at the two of them with an insistent *meow,* as though demanding to know what they were arguing about.

Cait absently rubbed the cat behind the ears. "All my life, you've talked about what it means to be a Fletcher. Now I want you to think about what it means. Would your own father be proud of the way you're behaving? Would Mum and Robbie? If I was the one lying there on the sofa, not willing to fight for my life, what would you be telling me?"

It was a dirty argument, but Cait was back in the glen now and fighting dirty was the only way she'd survived her teenage years. There were none of the politely vicious office politics of London here. When someone had something to say, they spoke their mind.

She pushed herself off the edge of the sofa and pointedly slid the soup closer to the edge. "Are you going to eat now or not?"

"I'll eat when I'm good and ready," he said, but he sat up. Picked the spoon off the table.

Letting him have the last word—at least about the soup—Cait took a few steps toward the door then paused. "Tonight's the tree lighting, don't forget," she said. "The weather site says it'll be bitter cold out, so you'll need to bundle up good and warm."

She held her breath, waiting for him to answer. He slurped his soup and let the spoon clatter back against the earthenware, part of a Staffordshire flow blue set that had come down in Cait's mother's family. "Nice try, but I've no intention of leaving the house. You let me be, now, Caitie. I mean it. I've no wish to keep arguing with you."

"You talk a lot for a man who doesn't want to argue."

"Only because you can't let anyone have an opinion that isn't the same as yours! You want to be useful, girl? Go fetch me my medicine from upstairs. Every one of my bones is aching."

Feeling helpless again, Cait brought him the medicine, took away the bowl when he'd eaten half the soup and insisted he wouldn't touch another drop, and tried to count the conversation a success.

On the bright side, for the first time in a long time, her father was being honest.

She went out to the kitchen to eat her own soup and clean up, and when she came back a half-hour later, he was asleep again, or pretending to sleep, so she took the opportunity to climb up to the attic. Brice hadn't exaggerated when he said he'd taken everything to the attic. He must have had help moving the furniture, and he'd stacked it along the walls, with everything else in boxes neatly marked by room.

Seeing the remnants of her mother's life all crammed up there, she finally sat down and allowed herself a good, hard cry. About that and about everything. Knees drawn to her chest, her back against an antique steamer trunk her mother had decorated with fashion lithographs from a torn 1850 copy of Court Magazine purchased at a jumble sale, Cait cried until she had no tears left.

Everywhere she turned, she found something that'd had meaning for her mother. In every box, she discovered a familiar picture, a scrap of fabric, a porcelain bit of bric-a-brac. Crammed all together the way the pieces were, the memories pummeled at Cait. Most were beautiful memories, warm ones, because her mother had been the constant thread of goodness woven throughout Cait's life. Goodness that had given Cait the space to be bad, to try and fail, to find herself. While Cait's father had been stern and a little remote with both his children, never quite accepting of Cait, Mum had always shown by example just what it meant to love someone. Shown that true love was bottomless and unconditional.

Thinking back on everything that had happened

since her mother's funeral, Cait couldn't help realizing she hadn't learned that lesson well enough.

If her mother had lived, she would never have let Cait run away. Not from Brice, nor the glen, nor from Donald. For all that Cait and Robbie had heard so much about what it meant to be a Fletcher, it wasn't the Fletcher side of the family that would help Cait get her father through his cancer. Or even to figure out her own mess of a relationship with Brice. All she had to do was remember the moments of her childhood, the small happy moments with her mother that had nothing to do with ambition or living a bigger life but simply added up to a life well-lived and well-loved. Both Cait and her father had been focusing so much on what they'd lost since Mum had died, they'd very nearly missed the fact that they'd had years of the kind of love many people spent entire lives without.

In London, there had been loneliness everywhere Cait looked, people chasing happiness too fast to catch it. She didn't know what to do about Brice—maybe only time would tell for the two of them. But a relationship wasn't everything. Being here in the glen was a gift in itself. Cait didn't know how to make her father feel less guilty about Robbie, but she could certainly show him that he was wrong about her mother. That he was wrong about her.

He would be disappointed in her decision to stay,

but he'd been disappointed in her most of her life. She would find a way to get through to him. She had to.

Even if the new sense of closeness she'd had with him this past year had been delusion on her part and deceit on his, being here, knowing that he was sick, made her realize she'd give anything to have that kind of a relationship be real between them. Fighting with him wasn't going to get her there. And as much as she hated to admit it, maybe the patience to accept the things that you couldn't do anything about required more courage than fighting anyway.

HOPES

"Hope is the thing with feathers
That perches in the soul
And sings the tune without the words
And never stops at all."

EMILY DICKINSON

A CHILL WIND SWEPT OFF THE LOCH, blowing the MacLaren hunting tartan of Brando's kilt around his knees. The cold froze Brice's breath on the sharp needles of the twelve-foot fir tree the two of them were carrying across the Inn's cobblestoned courtyard, but the moment they reached the corner where the village tree had been put up as far back as anyone could remember, the wind cut off.

The L-shaped Last Stand Inn looked vaguely Tudor, white-washed with age-darkened beams around the windows and a gabled roof, but it was both older than that and younger. Buildings and annexes and bits of courtyard and garden had grown from the original one-room structure throughout the centuries, and somehow, this one spot provided shelter from every direction, just about the only spot in the village where the wind didn't blow. Flora and Duncan Macara had already hung the traditional ball of mistletoe overhead nearby, suspended from a clothesline that extended from a second story window to the grand old hemlock that stood beside the fence. Brice had plans for that mistletoe later that evening.

Or more accurately, he had hopes.

He and Brando maneuvered the fir tree into its customary spot and slowly eased the trunk down onto the cobblestones. While Duncan hammered the base around it, they held it in place, and a few adjustments later, Flora Macara tipped her head, strolled all the way around the tree and pronounced it straight enough at last. The four of them stood back, and the small crowd that had filed out of the pub nursing their drinks clapped sporadically or whistled before shuffling back inside, their feet stamping on the mat as they blew on cold-reddened hands.

Brice rolled his shoulders and his aching neck. "Tell me again why I keep letting you rope me into volunteering for more work?"

"You're the one after redemption." Brando

clapped him on the back. "Are you out of shape now, mate, or what?"

"If you want a go at me, you've only to say the word."

"Naw. Thanks just the same," Brando said, grinning. "I learned that lesson a long while back. Anyway, I'll let Cait take you down a peg or two herself, now she's back. I can stand and watch and enjoy the show."

Brice wiped his palms on the rag he always kept in his back pocket while working at the garage. "Cait and I are good now. Or working our way in that direction. I hope."

Brando sent him a searching look. "You showed her the house, then, did you?"

"The house has nothing to do with it. The two of us have other matters to settle first."

"You're daft, man." Duncan, huddled like a tortoise inside of his roll neck sweater and anorak, stopped beside the two of them and frowned. "Here and you've been slaving away on that house for her these last eleven months. What are you waiting for?"

"The house is the topper, not the cake. I want Cait to believe in me without it."

"Aye, but it's nearly Christmas. Don't women love nothing better than a great, grand gesture? You leave it too long and anything could happen. Donald could send Cait running off back to London, and then where would you be?"

"Leave the boy alone, you great oaf." Flora strode toward the door to the Inn, her usual shapeless long skirt and drab, baggy sweater flapping around her. She rapped her husband's temple with her knuckles as she swept past. "What you know about women could fit on half a cocktail napkin, Duncan Macara. Can't think how I've put up with you all these years. Makes me wonder about myself sometimes."

Brando laughed. "*Why* you've put up with him is the bigger question."

The rest of them laughed, too, including Duncan, who raised his voice to call after his wife. "And I'm grateful you have, love. I truly am."

"Well, so you should be." Flora paused at the door and threw him a smile across her shoulder.

Her smile held so much love in it that Brice's heart went warm. Maybe he was getting soft himself with Cait back home at last, but it struck him that he'd have needed to search a fair distance to find a better example of love than Flora and her Duncan. On the surface, they were as mismatched a couple as anyone could find. Duncan, still handsome despite his gray hair and stooping shoulders, couldn't hold on to money to save his life, while Flora, plain-faced and raw-boned, wore clothes that had been washed and mended so often it was hard to imagine what they'd looked like originally. She wouldn't part with tuppence unless she had to, not unless Duncan had his heart set on some new toy or bit of nothing. Or unless someone—anyone—in the glen found themselves in need. But as ill-suited as those two were on the surface, Brice could only hope that he and Cait would fit as well together when they reached their sixties.

He hoped they would reach their sixties together.

It still sat oddly to have worries about their future. Here in the glen, love was seldom in doubt. A given. From the moment they were old enough to hope, men and women alike lined up on the bank of the loch on Beltane morning, waiting for the day the veil would lift away and the loch would show them the face of whoever they were meant to love. The gift of it took years, sometimes. Sometimes what was seen wasn't wanted. And hadn't *that* caused misery often enough?

Brice and Cait had never bothered looking. They'd never needed magic or a vision to tell them they were meant to be together, and all those years while others went down to the water, he and Cait had sat on the bank above, huddled in a blanket with their arms around each other, taking it for granted that they would build the future for themselves.

Brice had no intention of admitting to Cait that his faith hadn't lasted. This past year when things had seemed so bleak, though, he'd needed the reassurance the loch could offer. He'd lined up for the Sighting on the first of May along with half the village and busloads of tourists that Elspeth Murray's schemes and her American niece's planning skills had managed to lure up to the glen for the occasion. And in spite of centuries of village tradition and all the happiness and heartache he'd seen the Sighting cause in the glen as he grew up, he had stood there at the water's edge and found himself not quite believing. Then there Caitie had been, her face in the loch alongside his own as clearly as if she'd been on the bank beside him, so beautiful and dear it had been impossible to breathe.

He held that assurance close now, as he had all these long empty months without her. The promise that she'd come back to the glen, come back to him. Now that she was here, he had no intention of letting her slip away again.

That was why watching Flora and Duncan together warmed him, why he loved seeing how easily Brando and his fiancée Emma worked and laughed together. Brice hadn't had many examples of good relationships in his own life growing up. His mum had run off when he was six, and the last memory he had of her involved sitting on the corner of the old cracked bathtub before she'd gone, watching her slather layers of makeup over bruises his father's fists had left beneath her eyes.

Cait might have chewed the wrong end of the stick as far as Rhona Grewer was concerned the day she'd left him, but she hadn't been wrong to think he was out of line for drinking that afternoon. He'd been drunk enough not to care that it was Rhona raising a glass beside him, and that had been too much like the path his father had taken. Brice was nothing like his father. Yet it was all too easy to live down to expectations. He'd been doing it all his life. That was all Cait had ever known about him.

Looking up, he caught Flora watching him with her head tipped in contemplation. "You want my advice, Brice MacLaren?" she said from the threshold of the Inn, almost as though she'd heard what he was thinking. "Don't be afraid to give Cait time to follow her heart. She's a good girl. Always has been."

She pushed through the door and went inside, and the three men stared after her awkwardly until Duncan cleared his throat. "Why is it," he asked, "that women always think they know everything?"

"Usually because they do," Brando said.

"Aye, maybe," Duncan said, laughing and

sending cloudlets of breath into the air, but then he shook his head. "Take it from me, though, lad, and never let your Emma know it. Keep the moral high ground, that's the important thing, or you'll never survive with your sense of worth intact."

"I'd say the moral high ground is cold comfort compared to the warmth of a woman beside you," Brando retorted, eyeing Brice with a worried frown.

"We can all raise a pint to that, and to getting the village tree put up." Looping one arm around Brando's shoulder and another around Duncan's, Brice steered them toward the pub, though he knew his cousin well enough to suspect Brando had a lecture he meant to deliver. It had been Brando, after all, who'd picked Brice up after Cait had gone, who'd watched Brice trying to blame Cait, then Rhona, then Donald Fletcher—to blame anyone but himself— before he'd finally seen some sense. And Brando'd been the first to remind him that none of them were adolescents any longer, that if Brice wanted Cait or the rest of the village to take him seriously, he'd need to take himself more seriously first.

Which was a good reminder for the evening. Brice still had work to do. Reaching the door of the pub, it was tempting to go inside where the fire was warm and half the village had already stopped in for a pint before heading home to eat, but he stopped and turned the other way. The sun had dropped behind the braes already, casting crimson bands across the sky, and there was still the DB5 to detail before the tree lighting started at eight o'clock. He also needed to pick up more of the shelving from his house and drop it at the Tea Room.

He hadn't asked Cait if she was coming to the lighting, and he hadn't invited her. But he could hope that she'd be there.

He said goodnight to Brando and Duncan and started back across the cobblestones toward the gate and the lane where he'd left his Land Rover parked.

"You'll be careful with Cait, won't you?" Brando called after him. "It's not all about the two of you at the moment. She's got a lot to consider."

Brice turned back. "I know it. Which reminds me, it might ease her mind a bit if you'd consider finding a way to tell her you won't be selling pastries to Rhona Grewer once the Tea Room is open again."

"Even with the shop in Callander, I can't fully support two chefs," Brando said, ambling back to Brice and shaking his head. "Much as I wish business was that good. Emma needs the orders until she and Anna can get more events with catering on the books."

"So have her make a deal with Cait instead. Rhona did fine selling groceries and scones to go, and Cait was always good to you—"

"She was good to the both of us."

"Aye, and I was too stupid to see how lucky I was to have her."

Brando stepped forward and clapped him on the shoulder. "She's got a big heart, Cait does. She'll forgive you eventually."

"All I can do is the best I can," Brice said, "and hope that will be good enough."

CHANGES

THE CELEBRATION OF CHRISTMAS had only come
to the Highlands recently, or rather, the public
celebration of it had returned only in 1958. Whereas
the abolition of Christian feast days in the rest of
Britain had been long since repealed, in Scotland the
kirk had continued to frown on any observances that
went back to Roman Catholic traditions. Ironically,
here in the glen and in pockets of other out-of-the-way
places, even older celebrations had remained in place.
In Balwhither, the winter solstice and the approach of
Christmas still marked the cutting and lighting of the
Yule tree in the courtyard of the Inn, with candles of

hope for the return of the long, prosperous days and the remembrance of beloved friends and family lost, and a ball of mistletoe was cut each year from oaks on the hillside to symbolize the promise of new life after the long months of winter.

The occasion made Cait think of her mother again, for many reasons, as she parked the car and walked alone in the darkness toward the Inn. The courtyard blazed with light, and already voices were raised in song, though not yet the Christmas carols that would be led later by the members of Cait's old choir. These were rowdier drinking songs that went so well with the Highland coffees, spiced wine, warm grog, and hot Scotch toddies the Inn staff were passing around to the crowd gathered around the burning fire pots. Flames flickered gold over familiar faces, many of them people whom Cait hadn't seen since her mother's funeral.

Nerves slicked her palms with moisture and made her cold despite the layers in which she'd bundled herself before she'd left the house.

Still, it was better to get it over with. Like ripping a bandage off.

Smiling, she flicked the latch on the gate and went in, hoping most of the revelers would be too caught up in the occasion to notice her.

Elspeth Murray saw her straight away. Splitting

away from a group that included her American niece, Emma, who'd come to the glen and married Connal MacGregor of Inverlochlarig House down at the end of the long glen road, Elspeth hurried toward Cait and pushed her arm through Cait's elbow to draw her forward. "There you are," she said. "I was so hoping you would come. Hoped you could talk your father into coming as well, but I suppose we can't have everything. Not yet anyway." Leaning closer, she added in Cait's ear, "Now don't you go letting yourself get nervous. Or caught up in sadness. This is a night for celebration. Everyone here will be remembering the last time they saw you, too, and they've already heard what Donald's done. No one blames you for his decisions."

Cait let herself be pulled deeper into the courtyard, returning the smiles and hugs and hands held out to greet her. Vision blurring just a little, she swallowed hard and blinked the moisture back, grateful to be home as the choir, dressed for the occasion in long white robes, took their places on one side of the tree.

In the midst of it all, Cait found herself, suddenly, standing in front of Brando MacLaren and a sweet-faced blond woman who she assumed must be the other American—the fiancée Brando had found for himself in Cornwall. The two of them were chatting with Anna MacGregor and her step-daughter, Moira. Brando, dressed in his usual kilt, boots, and leather jacket over a thick knitted sweater, swept Cait up and around and around and kissed her soundly on the cheek before setting her down again.

"It's a sight for sore eyes, you are," he said as Emma looked on, smiling shyly. "If you'd stayed away any longer, I'd have needed to come and drag you back from London myself. Have you met Emma, yet? The two of you should talk if you're going to open the Tea Room back up again. She's brilliant at making pastries, and we'd rather sell to you than to Rhona, if you'd find a use for something ready-made."

Cait hugged Emma warmly. "Congratulations on taming the kilted beast," she said. "You should know you've broken every feminine heart from here to Inverness—and I'd love to talk about pastries once I have my feet back under me a bit."

"Any time," Emma said. "Come up to the hotel for lunch. Or dinner."

Moira MacGregor, her lovely, elfin face still mildly lopsided from facial palsy she'd been born with, ran to Cait and threw her arms around her. "Does that mean you're opening the library again, Cait?" she asked. "Say you are."

Cait squeezed Moira back, thinking of how many times her own mum had held her just like this, thinking how uncomplicated things were when you were Moira's age. On the other hand, Moira had never let her courage fail her. Or lashed out at anyone unfairly.

Cait's own doubts and nerves vanished just like that. "Absolutely," she said to Moira. "What would the Tea Room be without the books?"

"There. You see?" Her face shining, Moira turned to Anna, who came to hug Cait, too, and though the two of them hadn't had much time to get to know each other before Cait had left for London, Cait had always found herself drawn to Anna's kindness and the little kernel of self-doubt she'd thought she glimpsed sometimes when Anna's guard was down. A void of confidence that Cait had recognized in herself.

Of course, their circumstances were very different these days. Anna had married Connal MacGregor whose grandfather and grandmother, in turn, had been Chiefs of the clan MacGregor, making Connal the closest thing the glen had to a laird these days.

"And where's Himself then?" Cait asked, looking around for the man, because in all the years he'd lived in the glen he'd never allowed himself to be far from his daughter, as much as he hated being out in the public eye.

"He'll slip in quietly once the lighting is underway. That's our compromise these days, now that the tabloid interest has mostly died down," Anna said. "The paparazzi seem to have finally gotten used to the idea that he's a settled family man with no intention of going back to acting. Still, he worries."

She didn't specify what caused the worry, but then she didn't need to spell it out. Both she and Cait glanced down at Moira, whose fey, delicate features and long silvery hair increasingly resembled those of her famous mother, the actress Isobel Teague. Connal's first wife had been every bit as famous as Connal himself, and her death in a car accident had haunted Connal until he met and fell in love with Anna. Let himself fall in love with Anna.

Self-inflicted wounds, Cait decided, were so often the hardest ones to heal.

The thought was a bitter one made even harder to swallow as she spotted Brice walking toward her carrying a cup in either hand. It was strange how coming home again was making her aware of wounds she hadn't even known she had inside her.

"I'm glad you came," Brice said, stopping beside her. He handed her a cup of the spiced wine that she had always loved and kept the other for himself.

"I wasn't going to come," she admitted, gesturing

around her, "but I've missed this. Remember how much we used to complain about being dragged out for all these village events? Now they're among the things that make me thankful to be back again."

She shifted uncomfortably as he searched her face, the fire in the nearby pot turning the amber rings around his honey brown irises to molten gold, and she could see the questions he was holding back, the sudden awkwardness and distance that stood between them. There was a time he would have said what he was thinking—a time when he wouldn't have needed to say it aloud.

That was the most startling realization of all: that Brice had become someone she didn't know anymore. But she wanted to know him.

She drew the cup of wine to her lips and took a cautious sip. It had cooled to the perfect temperature, tangy with orange juice, cardamom, cinnamon, and star anise. Heaven when her limbs felt cold and her throat felt dry.

"Thanks for this," she said. "It's perfect."

"I remember."

They both turned away as Duncan Macara stepped up to the makeshift platform that was used for so many of the village events and rang the bell to get everyone's attention. He'd put on one of the ugliest of his Christmas sweaters, a red one with a tree that extended from collar to waist, hand-embroidered in long, awkward stitches and decorated with tiny pompom ornaments.

"Welcome, all," he said. "We'll be passing around the candles and holders while the choir sings. Once you have yours, come up to the tree, oldest of us to youngest, same as ever. And thanks to Brando and Brice for finding this beautiful tree and bringing it to us. Thanks to old friends and the new ones among us, to those returning and those who've gone. May the winter nights be mild and quickly gone, and may the summer days come soon to warm us."

"May the summer days come soon," everyone said at once, lifting their cups and glasses.

Cait watched Anna gently wipe chocolate and whipped cream from Moira's upper lip, remembering her own mother doing the same. And though she'd never given much thought to having children of her own, the yearning to see her father hold her child, to see the next generation born, nearly doubled her over suddenly.

Not that *that* was likely to happen.

She tried to think of Brice as father material. Tried not to look at him.

Tried not to think of the two of them together at all—because they weren't.

A kilted Iain Camm MacGregor stepped up to the platform beside Duncan and brought the reed of his bagpipes to his lips. The long wheeze of the initial notes gave way to the haunting melody of "Silent Night," bringing goosebumps to Cait's forearms, because the sound of the pipes, too, was something that she had missed in London. When the song was done, spry little Jenny Lawrence, a scarlet hat pulled low over her sparse white hair, raised her conductor's baton and set the choir into singing "The Holly and the Ivy."

The tray of clips and small white candles passed by Cait's elbow. She took one of each, then waited her turn as each of the villagers lit their candles and carried them, hands cupped around wavering flames, over to the beautiful fir that Brando and Brice had cut in the woods earlier that day. And the fact that Brice had done that was yet another reminder that he had changed. Brando had been working hard for years to change his reputation in the glen. No job had been beneath him. Cait had taken his example a bit herself, but Brice had never bothered.

Climbing up onto the stepladder, she searched for a spot in the branches and stretched to clip her candle high up on the tree. She wobbled unexpectedly, and hands gripped her waist as someone steadied her.

When she looked behind her, she wasn't surprised to find Brice there.

"Careful, love," he said.

It was a good reminder. One she needed.

Brice's touch, his face, everything about him was at once dangerously familiar and unknown. It made her forget that everything was different. That she needed a miracle just to hold on to the little bit of familiarity, of family, that she had left.

But as she clipped her candle on the branch, the wavering flame of the candle steadied in the curious lack of wind that happened around the tree for the lighting each year. The flame slowly lengthened, burning with the others and forming stars of light in her stinging eyes.

Cait needed only to look at the tree, at all the unwavering candle flames burning like miniature beacons, for proof that miracles existed. In the glen, there were still wee bits of magic now and again to remind those who lived here that there was something much larger than any single person, than any single life.

She started to climb down the stepladder again, but Brice put his hands around her waist and lifted her, turning her around by the shoulders once her feet had touched the ground. Cait didn't need to look up to be aware that they stood directly beneath the ball of mistletoe strung on the line that stretched above the courtyard. Her heart began to pound, as much in anticipation as from the feel of his arms around her. From the warmth of his eyes on hers as he slowly bent his head.

She wanted to close her eyes, but she couldn't look away.

He didn't kiss her, though. Instead, he only brushed her cheek with his lips and left her feeling cold and lonely.

COURTING

*"Maybe...you'll fall in love
with me all over again."*

ERNEST HEMINGWAY
A FAREWELL TO ARMS

C AIT WAS ASTONISHED AT HOW HER PLANS for the photographs galvanized the glen. News spread, and over the next two days, she had a stream of visitors both at the house and at the Tea Room. Women who had scarcely spoken ten words to Cait in her entire life drank tea at her kitchen table and entrusted her with photographs and paintings of the women in their families so that she could scan and print off copies to hang on the Tea Room walls.

They brought a story with every photograph, telling them with pride and tears and laughter. The stories were as varied as the one about a MacLaren great aunt who had saved her brother from drowning in the loch, or a MacGregor grandmother who'd put money by, a penny and a pound at a time, to see a grandson off to America for a better life. There were stories from the wars, and between the wars, women who farmed the land themselves, repaired roofs, raised children alone. Ran abusive husbands off with shotguns. Older stories went back as far as the time of the massacre of eighteen MacLaren men by MacGregor men—though how that story went varied depending on who told it. Then there were the women, like Rob Roy MacGregor's wife Mary, who'd done their best to ward off cattle raids or English soldiers with nothing more than flintlock muskets and the valiant dog who tended their sheep and slept beside their hearths at night.

Life in the Highlands had always been harsh. The landscape was heavy with grief and history and appropriately overcast skies, soaked in the blood of those who died for their homes, their kin, or their beliefs. That made it a breeding ground for heroes, male and female. The thought fired Cait's imagination. She'd never considered her home in those terms growing up, in spite of the romantic notions of the tourists gleaned from films and the stories of authors like Robert Louis Stephenson or Walter Scott. More and more, as she listened to the individual stories brought to her, she saw the history of the glen as a patchwork of small victories and defeats and not just part of the bigger picture. It made her realize there were heroes in every family, in every country around the world. Heroes forgotten because younger generations weren't interested until the chance to hear the individual stories had long since passed.

It was that thought that drove her to type the stories frantically with her imagination working overtime. It drove her, too, back to the sitting room to sit with her father as often as she could, no matter how much he protested. Between visitors and sorting her mother's things in the attic and repainting in the Tea Room, she told him about what she was doing, told him about her plans, told him the stories she was hearing. Coaxing him to talk was even harder than trying to keep her distance from Brice, though. Increasingly worried, she spoke to the doctor again several times, but while he urged her to get her father back to his office, he didn't offer much help in suggesting how to accomplish that. Or how to force her father to have a procedure he didn't want. Apart from giving her the contact information for the Depression Alliance, he didn't offer much at all. Cait dragged her own bed into her father's bedroom, threw the shades open and washed the windows both there and downstairs to try and let in some of the weak winter sunshine, and she brewed St. John's Wort with his tea to lift his mood. She played Whist and Cribbage with him in between his naps when he was willing. None of which seemed to help.

"He's like a hibernating bear," she told Brice out of pure frustration when they were both working at the Tea Room on Friday afternoon. "Curled up and waiting for something. Waiting for death to come. I don't know what to do with him. He said more to me in any single phone conversation we had this past year than he's said to me the whole time since I've been home. Even last week he was chatting on the phone to me for twenty minutes at a stretch. I've been over those conversations in my head a hundred times trying to figure out what I missed."

Brice pulled a finished shelf off the sawhorses and gestured for Cait to take the opposite end so they could carry it to the wall and she could hold it steady while he screwed the bracket in. "It's easy to put in an effort for twenty minutes. He probably can't face the idea of having to do it all day long."

"He can't seem to face anything. I try to tell him what I'm doing with the Tea Room, and he doesn't care. He's not interested in what I feed him or what I do. The only time I get any kind of a reaction out of him is when I try to turn the telly off. Oh, and when I mentioned bringing something down from the attic, he bit my head off. I know he's in pain, and it's not that I want to make him live with that. But the pain will only get worse, from what the doctor says, and it doesn't need to. Dad refuses to discuss any of that. He pretends to sleep just so I'll stop talking."

"So stop talking, then," Brice said, raising an eyebrow at her as she held a shelf level for him to screw in place. "Wait him out."

"Every day we wait gives the cancer more of a chance to take hold. And it isn't as though I'm nagging at him. I've been trying to be careful about that when it comes to anything but eating. He's like you in that way, the more I bring something up, the more he'll do the opposite."

Grinning, Brice drove the screw into the bracket with the electric drill. "Sweetheart, if that's not the pot accusing the kettle, I'll take a swim in the loch come Christmas morning."

Cait stuck her tongue out at him as he tested the bracket to make sure it didn't wiggle. Then, slowly, he walked down the length of the shelf to where she stood and stopped so close every nerve in her body awoke. The look in his eye made her catch her breath.

He had only to look at her and she caught fire; that

much had never changed. These past two days, though, he'd refused to do more than that, as if he knew that it would drive her mad.

"What ever happened to your idea of courting me, by the way?" she asked. "I hope this isn't the best you can do?"

He grinned again and winked at her. Then he pulled the other bracket from the pocket of his jeans and positioned it beneath her end of the shelf. The drill's motor whined as he fastened it in, one screw and then the other, sending up a faint whiff of fresh paint and sawdust. Only when he'd finished did he look at her again.

"If you're not sure whether I'm courting you, *mo chridhe*, you haven't been paying attention," he said.

"Or maybe you're not working hard enough." She stepped a little closer. "Maybe you're not doing it right."

He reached for her finally, slowly. But his hand stopped before it reached her face and only brushed a bit of sawdust from her shoulder. His eyes were dancing with amusement. "Courting's not all about sex and kissing, or haven't you heard? Maybe that's the whole point I'm making. It's never been the physical side that's been a problem between us."

"True," she said, her voice coming out too thin and strangled until she cleared her throat and tried again. "So what are you doing, then? What are *we* doing?"

"We're getting to know each other. Learning to trust each other all over again."

She bit her lip and stared down at the distorted shadows the two of them were casting on the floor. It was impossible to keep looking at him directly. "How long do you suppose that will take?"

His expression sobered into something that was serious with a wistful edge. "Maybe you'll tell me when you're ready. When you know me. When you know yourself. For my part, I've known all I need to know about you since I was ten."

Her eyes darted back to his, but he gave her no clue how to answer. In the end, she realized she was still standing there like an idiot, holding up a shelf that was now fully supported by brackets on both ends. He'd stepped back and stood watching her, so she only nodded and went back over to pick up the paintbrush and the wall stencil she had made from cutout cardboard, climbed up on her stepladder, and resumed her painting.

He threw the next shelf on the sawhorses and started going over it with the sander, whistling cheerfully. Feeling entirely wrong-footed and off balance, she wished she'd never brought up the subject of courting at all. How had he managed to change the rules of flirting? The whole dynamic between them?

Then again, he was changing everything. And there was truth, too, in what he'd said.

She couldn't deny that anymore. She had never for a moment fallen out of love with Brice; she doubted she ever could. Loving someone and being able to live with them, on the other hand, being able to keep that love from turning the corner into hate and disappointment, that was something else. The Brice she had left in the glen had been exciting, thrilling. He'd been kind and intelligent, clever in many different ways. But he had never been the sort of man that she would have been able to count on for the day to day of fifty or sixty years.

That was the biggest change of all. Each morning when she came to work in the Tea Room, he was here working already, or he'd already been and gone. Before she had even been able to tell him not to bother with the paint, he'd driven down to Edinburgh and brought it back for her, en route to getting back nearly all the library books that he'd left there for consignment, which he'd had to rent a truck and bring back in two trips. He'd even found her an entire crate of old wooden picture frames in a variety of styles and shapes and sizes that she knew would look wonderful on the walls with the copied photos of women from around the glen. He'd been the one to find the scanner and printer for her, too, as a loan from Anna MacGregor who'd gotten them in for her work managing events for Brando's restaurant and hotel. All of this Brice had done without a fuss or fanfare, which was another change from the old Brice she'd known. That younger Brice had done plenty of lovely, thoughtful things for her through the years they'd been together, but he'd expected acknowledgment and praise for them all.

RESPECT

*"If you want to be respected by others,
the great thing is to respect yourself."*

FYODOR DOSTOYEVSKY
THE INSULTED AND HUMILIATED

CAIT TRIED SO HARD TO MASK HER FRUSTRATION
that Brice couldn't help hoping his plan was
working. She had to come to him on her own, to
decide she wanted to come to him. He couldn't be the
one to chase her.

The logic was sound. From what he'd seen, Cait
had yet to even question why she had chosen to give
up on him so easily, why she had left the glen. As
focused as she was on her father now, he couldn't
know whether she was looking at Brice as a diversion,
or something familiar, a crutch. He was happy to be
all those things, but he didn't want her to regret it. He

didn't want for her to leave again.

The one thing he knew for certain was that their old relationship had been based on patterns and feelings they'd established when he and Cait had both been too young, too troubled. Those sorts of patterns couldn't form the basis for a solid relationship, not the kind of relationship that would be healthy and satisfying now. Which meant that the relationship had to change.

Still, even knowing that, having Cait here beside him without touching her was harder than he'd imagined. Having her back again was still a constant surprise, one that brought a surge of joy every time he saw her. He wanted to hold her, itched to brush the dark silk of her hair away from her face, ached to kiss the lips she wanted him to kiss. Aye, and he felt her wanting that, too. He knew her well enough to be sure of that.

But patience was another way in which he'd changed. He'd lived without Cait for fifteen long months. A few days—a few months, if need be—more would be worth the wait.

In the meantime, he'd been taking pleasure in helping her in the Tea Room. That was something he could do. After the first room where they'd done it out of sequence and had to paint the walls *around* the shelves, now he was waiting until Cait had the base color back on the walls in each room the way she wanted before he fastened the new bookshelves in place. He helped with the paint as well, though he took care to make sure she didn't know it. She'd always been brilliant at detail, like the beautiful wall stencils she had cut out of cardboard and was painting around the ceilings, windows, and door frames in all the rooms, but when it came to the less showy work of creating a smooth surface on the walls themselves, of laying a foundation instead of creating the embellishments, she didn't have the patience. He waited until she'd gone home each night and came back and touched up the mottled spots where she hadn't laid the paint down evenly and corrected the places where she'd gotten color on the ceiling or the trim.

He'd learned to appreciate the slow work of painting more and more himself. In fact, he realized on the morning of Christmas Eve as he watched his client inspect the finished DB5, it was work itself that he'd come to appreciate, the opportunity to do every aspect of a project well.

The client, a balding Edinburgh banker in his forties with more money than he knew how to spend, stood beside Brice and peered down into the engine, then closed the bonnet and ran a hand over the silk smooth paint that Brice had painstakingly laid down in the booth layer by layer. There wasn't a single thing on the car that called attention, only the beauty of the whole. Maybe relationships were like that, too, Brice thought. Not about one person or the other, but about what they could become together.

He buffed out the trace of engine grease the man had left on the silver paint then handed the man the faded red rag to wipe his hands. "You like it?"

"It's even better than I'd hoped," the client said, running the rag across his fingertips. "To be frank, I wasn't entirely sure you could pull it off, but you don't see many of these come up for sale. I had to take the chance. You're still willing to do the XJ220 for me?"

"If I can find one," Brice said. "I'll start looking after Christmas."

The client dug a folded cashier's check out of his wallet and handed it over. Brice refrained from examining it there and then, pretended that his mouth hadn't gone dry and his heart wasn't pounding. The keys were in the ignition already, so he only opened the door so the client could slide in behind the wheel and pull away, followed by his bored looking wife in a far less flashy Bentley.

The two cars kicked up dust as they braked at the end of the drive and turned off toward the village. It was only when they were out of sight that Brice allowed himself to unfold the check and look at it. Just look. Glad he had given the rest of his crew time off for the holiday, he slumped back against the wall, still staring. Oblivious to everything but the numbers until Brando pulled into the drive in Emma's little Volvo and got out.

"Car didn't want to turn over this morning. I had to jump it for her," he said. "Do you have a minute to take a look?"

Brice gave himself a mental shake. "Sure. No problem."

"Something wrong?" Brando closed the Volvo's door and came around. "You're standing here looking like someone shot your feet out from under you." Peering down, he whistled as he caught sight of the check before Brice had thought to put it away. "You didn't say that car was worth so much. Hell, I could buy a whole new hotel for that. Or half the glen."

"Would have been worth more if all the parts were original. I had to put in a few remanufactured pieces, though. Still, it turned out all right."

The look Brando threw him said he knew Brice better than that. "You mind having to watch it drive out of here with someone else?"

"What would I do with a car like that? I'm not exactly a man of leisure."

"Shame, though," Brando said. "You could keep the next one. Why not? The house is nearly finished, isn't it? And you used to talk my ear off about that car when we were growing up."

Brice thought back to the days when he'd dreamed of racing into the village in a James Bond car. He'd pictured himself screeching to a halt, casually getting out, and ignoring the admiring glances, the way everyone envied him. Respected him. But it had been James Bond he'd dreamed of being back then, not just Brice MacLaren in a fancy car. Thinking of restoring a car like the DB5 for himself, he realized that somewhere along the line, between that first junked clunker he'd bought for fifty pounds and sold for five hundred to the Aston Martin that was his most ambitious to date by far, his priorities had changed. The restoration wasn't only about making money anymore, or even about the cars. It was the work itself, the process of taking something and watching it transform beneath his hands. It was about the pride.

He wished he could have shown Cait the DB5, not just to show her that he had accomplished something, that—someday—he'd be able to give her the world and anything it took to make her happy, but just to show her that he could plan, and build, and work up to something. He'd briefly considered driving the car up to her house and asking her casually to come with him for a spin, leaving it parked in the drive so that Donald could see as well. It would have felt a bit too much like a cat dropping a dead mouse at her feet, though. Too much like begging for approval.

Same reason he couldn't see keeping a car like that for himself now, come to think of it.

Or one of them anyway.

"The bank is still due a chunk of this check now that I've been paid," he said, "and another bit has to go toward finishing the house. Then I'll need the rest to buy the next car and start that restoration."

"I take it Cait still doesn't have a clue what you've been doing?"

Brice stuffed the check back into his pocket. "Not unless someone else has told her. I wasn't planning to show her the house yet, either, not until it was completely finished, but I'm thinking I'll bring her and Donald around for dinner tonight. They haven't even got a tree of their own put up. Donald insists he doesn't want her to make a fuss."

"I thought he'd promised to go down to London to celebrate with her."

"He had, but I'm not convinced he ever meant it. He's been worse since she came home than I've ever seen him. Trying to drive her away, whether he knows it or not, I expect."

Brando made a face. "Get Cait a tree, then. That's my advice, or she'll be miserable waking up tomorrow with no sign of Christmas. Her mum always made it an occasion."

"With or without a tree, it won't be very festive. The house is still bare as a bairn's bottom, and I know it pains her to have all of Morag's things hidden away up in the attic."

"I'm surprised she's left them there. That's not much like Cait at all." Brando looked thoughtfully at Brice. "They'll both be down here for dinner tonight? You're certain of it?"

"Nothing's certain with Donald, but I mean to try."

"Then let me have your key to Donald's house. I'll get Rory and Angus and Iain Camm around, and the three of us will bring everything back down from the attic. Put the house back as it was. Elspeth Murray can help me figure out where it all should go, and we'll put a tree up for Cait while we're at it. She's had a hard enough time of it lately."

"Donald would kill the lot of us for that." Brice rubbed a hand across the back of his neck, but he wasn't going to get Donald's approval no matter how he tried. Cait was the one who mattered. "Might do the old mule a world of good to give a thought to his daughter instead of wallowing in his own misery. Aye, it's a good idea. I'll get him out of that house tonight if I have to drag him by the ears."

APOLOGIES

*"I am the wisest man alive,
for I know one thing,
and that is that I know nothing."*

PLATO
THE REPUBLIC

C AIT DARED TO BRING DOWN ONLY TWO THINGS
from the attic, given her father's state of mind: a
locket of her mother's containing a photograph of
Robbie holding a newborn Cait that her father had
promised to give to her when he found it, and the book
of her mother's family recipes. She was in the kitchen
baking one of the shortbread variations into the shape
of a Christmas tree, or trying to anyway, when Brice
came to the door and gave two peremptory knocks
before opening it and stepping through.

With a delighted *mrrow*, Mrs. Bogan wound

herself around his legs, insisting as usual that anyone new to her sphere of influence pay her the proper homage. "Don't mind Mrs. Bogan," Cait said, since the two had yet to be properly introduced. "She's a bit of a trollop, but be warned. The moment you pet her, she'll expect you to be her slave for life."

"Is that a cat trait or a feminine one?" Brice asked, stooping nevertheless to rub the top of Mrs. Bogan's head. "No, don't answer that."

Cait dusted her hands and turned to face him. "I know I've been pushing you hard to help me in the Tea Room—taking up a lot of your time. I want to apologize for that. The fact is, Dad should never have asked you to help him renovate it in the first place, and I feel like I'm taking advantage of you, too."

"That wasn't what I meant. And I offered to do the shelves, remember? I'm enjoying the work." Brice dropped his eyes and took in Cait's appearance, making her self-conscious suddenly of the flour streaked across her jumper as he grinned in amusement. "You look like whatever you're making has gotten the better of you," he said. "I hear tell there's this thing called an apron a person can wear over their clothes."

"Maybe I'll buy myself one for Christmas. All of Mum's are stored away. Which is a bit ironic actually, since she never seemed to need one. I can't imagine how she didn't manage to get dirty while she was baking. Clearly, that's a talent I didn't inherit from her."

"You have other talents. But actually, it's cooking I came to see you about." Brice shut the door and leaned back against it. "My cooking, not yours. I have a dinner invitation for you."

There was an uncertainty about the way he said the words, about the slight waver in his smile, that made Cait suspect the invitation wasn't as casual as his tone made it sound. "An invitation to what?" she asked. "Something important?"

He slid his hands down into the front pockets of his jeans. "It's important to me. I'd like to have you and your father come for dinner tonight. And before you think of saying no, I've already got the roast in the oven and Brando's Emma made a Christmas cake for you. Think how sad it would be if I had to eat all that myself."

"Dad won't come." Cait went to wash her hands, buying time until she thought she could trust her voice. "He's determined not to celebrate Christmas this year."

Brice peeled himself away from the door and straightened. "If I can get him to change his mind, will you come?" He cleared his throat and watched her. "I hate to think of you here on your own—or working in the Tea Room after he's gone to bed. You used to love it when your mum made a big deal of Christmas Eve."

Cait tried not to wince. Not to feel the loneliness and loss that had been threatening to squeeze her lungs closed all day at the thought of being in the house tonight with only her memories for company. "I thought I'd work on the photographs tonight. I don't know what I'm going to do with them yet, but I'm typing up all the stories to go with them. And I've got nice fish to fry up with a caper sauce for Dad."

"Fish would make a fine first course." Brice gave her his best let-me-lead-you-into-temptation smile. "All I'm asking is that you let me speak to him about it," he said. "Come on, Caitie. Don't sell me short. You know I can be persuasive."

How many things had Brice talked Cait into through the years? Too many. She remembered that smile, the way he whispered in her ear. Kissed the corner of her mouth.

"I warn you, your usual persuasion techniques will be wasted on my father," she said, taking a self-protective step backwards. "But go ahead. I'll enjoy watching you try."

Brice flashed her a triumphant grin and scooped up Mrs. Bogan, rubbing the cat beneath the chin as he strode through the kitchen and out to the sitting room where Cait's father was watching an old documentary about the Knights Templar, complete with conspiracy theories, hidden treasure, and reenactments of men bashing each other with swords. Rather than lying down on the sofa, however, Donald was sitting up with his leg propped on a cushion Cait had set on the table for him. Which was not much of an improvement, but it was something. Cait counted every hint of progress as a victory these days.

"I'd like to have you and Cait in for dinner tonight," Brice said. "It would mean a lot if you'd come."

"I'm not hungry." Donald glanced at him then returned his focus to the television.

"It's hours away yet."

"Won't be hungry later, either," Donald said.

Brice crossed the sitting room and mashed the power button on the set. The room grew mercifully quiet. "Cait's under the impression that you don't care enough about her to make an effort for Christmas," he said, "but I told her she had to be wrong. That Donald Fletcher couldn't possibly be as selfish as that with his own daughter."

"I never said any of that," Cait said, outraged.

Her father's face went red. "Don't think you can play games with me, Brice MacLaren. You're not half as clever as you think you are—and you always were insufferable. No better than your father for all you've been swanning around here pretending." He pointed at Brice with a shaky finger. "Don't think I don't see through you, trying to worm yourself into my good graces. You stay away from Cait, you hear me? She's not going to let herself get caught up with the likes of you again."

He'd said similar things to Brice dozens of times through the years, and worse. The kind of things that had made Brice storm out of the house and made Cait run after him, made Cait run wild with him in the glen, until her mother managed, somehow, to smooth things over. Being compared to his father was the thing Brice had always hated most, the thing that had triggered the worst of his rages and set him off to find a bottle of Mad Mackenzie's finest. This time, Brice barely reacted, and only a hint of stiffness in his shoulders and the little line at the corner of his mouth revealed that he still felt the barb hit home.

Cait snatched up the television remote from the table where her father was in the process of reaching for it. "Brice isn't fourteen anymore," she said. "You can't bully him to make yourself feel better—especially after all he's done for you. As kind as he's been."

"He didn't do any of it for me, though, did he?"

Her father threw Brice a contemptuous look. "Don't you think I've seen through him all along? Thinking he could win me over to get you back."

"So you *used* him?"

Her father snapped his fingers. "Give me that remote. Or turn the telly back on. I'm missing my show."

"Not until you apologize to Brice."

"Why should I? How much misery did he cause *me* through the years? Arguments with you, with your mother. Never a day's peace in this house since the first time I got called in to pick you up at school with everyone watching. And the shame of it. You're a Fletcher, Cait. You've no cause to be taking up with the likes of him. Not when you're meant for better things."

"Enough!" Brice's voice was loud enough to make Mrs. Bogan flatten her ears and jump out of his arms. "Enough blame and enough sulking," he said, coming to stand beside Cait. He slipped an arm around her waist. "It's a tragedy what's happened to you, we all see that. Cancer's tragic and painful and hard, but we've all spent more than enough time letting you be unreasonable and petty and mean because you're feeling sorry for yourself. And you see what you're doing, don't you? Refusing to celebrate Christmas now is only going to make Cait doubt you ever intended to celebrate in London with her."

"You don't know what you're talking about." Cait's father folded his arms like a five-year-old and glared at Brice.

Brice shook his head. "Look, I'm not asking you to do anything strenuous. You can lay on the sofa at my house as easily as on this one, and I've got a telly same as you. Think of Cait for a change. Don't make her spend Christmas cooped up here with you—the way you're going, that's worse than if she were by herself."

"No one's stopping her from leaving." Leaning forward, Donald grabbed for the television remote Cait was holding.

Cait snatched it out of reach. "I'm not going anywhere without you, and you bloody well know it."

"It won't be as simple as dinner," Donald muttered. "You haven't learned a thing if that's what you think. But aye, fine. I'll go if you'll stop nagging at me and let me get back to watching my show in peace. I only hope he can manage to make something halfway edible."

"Why do you have to say things like that?" Cait asked, fed up—beyond fed up. "Brice doesn't deserve it, and I don't, either."

"I'm not apologizing to him."

Cait went and sat down on the sofa beside him. "All my life, you've talked about being a Fletcher," she said more quietly, "as if that's supposed to mean something. But who we are isn't about what some long-ago ancestor has done. It's about us. About not letting Mum or Robbie down and diminishing how they lived their lives. They were never mean, either of them. They lived their whole lives with courage and kindness. They respected other people."

"I kept a roof over your head—"

"Aye, you gave me a roof and the food on my table, but Mum would have done that if you hadn't. When you bring a bairn into the world, that's the minimum you owe them. But don't you think you owe them love, too, and pride in their accomplishments?"

Her father pulled his bad leg off the cushion on the table and swiveled to study her. "You think I'm not proud of you? That I don't love you?"

"I don't know," Cait said, her voice unsteady. "Do you?"

"Of course I do. I always have."

"Then stay with me, try to *want* to stay with me, the way you'd want to stay with Mum or Robbie."

"Cait—"

"No. Stop. You're all I have left. Can't you see that? So what if you end up with half a leg? Jeff

Glasbrenner and Arunima Sinha both climbed Mount Everest with a prosthetic below the knee. And Mark Inglis reached the summit with *two* prosthetics. Are you really telling me you're not willing to try to climb the stairs in your own house because it would be too hard? I don't believe that for a minute. I used to think you were the strongest man I knew. I looked up to you. So did Robbie. Either both of us were wrong or—like I said—I'm just not important enough to you."

She was crying now, hating herself for it. But how was she supposed to get through to him?

He sat staring at her, his big hands splayed on his thighs as if he was bracing himself to stand up. When he didn't move, didn't say anything, Brice sat down beside her and pulled her against his chest while she cried, his chin resting against her hair.

"Shh, love. It's all right," he said.

"But it isn't, is it?"

"It will be."

Cait's father cleared his throat. "Fine, so dinner, then. Five o'clock, you said? But I won't wear a tie."

"Come in your pajamas for all I care." Brice sounded relieved, then he added with a smile that Cait could hear in his voice, "Come to think of it, I think Cait gave you Christmas pajamas once."

Cait gave a hiccup of watery laugher. "Aye, and they had moose on them wearing Santa hats. I'd forgotten about those."

Brice kissed the top of her head and stepped away. "See you tonight, then."

She stood at the front window while he climbed in the Land Rover. The engine revved, the wheels spun an instant, and he backed out onto the road.

Down the hill below him, Flora Macara was chasing Shame behind the Inn, the yellow dog dropping down to his belly and letting her get to within a few feet before he bounded away again. Throughout the glen, smoke from the chimneys rose in the air, and the snow on the braes made the most of the descending winter sun. It was so beautiful, so familiar and dear and so much a part of herself, that it made Cait want to throw her arms wide and embrace it all.

"You need to know," her father said, hobbling up behind her. "It wasn't that I didn't mean to come down to you for Christmas."

She turned away from the window, but he met her eyes only briefly then went to stand beside her looking down into the glen.

"I kept telling myself I'd feel better," Donald continued slowly, as if the words were painful, "and the more it sank in that I never would, the more I couldn't seem to make myself do anything to acknowledge it. You get the feeling it all has to be a mistake, something like cancer. Then I realized, maybe it could be a blessing in disguise." He tightened his grip on the cane, his knuckles white and his hand trembling, and darted a glance at her. "I should have told you, though. I know that, and the fact that I didn't shames me. I should have said I didn't have the strength to come to London or the heart to celebrate anything. I never set out to let you down, Caitie. It was hard enough last year when we were together to keep you from seeing how much the memories were wearing on me. I knew I couldn't manage it this time around. I had too much to hide."

"You never let me see how hard it was last year," she said carefully. "I thought we had a good time together."

"We did." He nodded and finally turned to face her. "We did. And I've never meant to make you feel as if you matter less than Robbie. Rob was always easy. Like your mum. And I knew the things to teach him, to say to him. The things my father said to me. But I didn't have sisters, and you weren't easy. From the day you were born, you were as prickly as a box of hedgehogs. I'd tell you something, and you'd ask me for an explanation. Or a reason. Or you'd have your own idea. You always had an opinion."

"Like you."

He smiled faintly. "Aye, maybe. Like me, I suppose. Maybe that's why we've always butted heads, but it's never meant I love you less."

He'd never said anything like that before. Hearing the words, Cait felt as if a weight had lifted, one that had been pressing on her for so long she'd forgotten it was there. Her throat tight and aching, she said, "Can we start with a fresh slate, then?"

Her father put both hands on his cane and leaned heavily against it, but he managed to smile at her. "I'd like that. Only I'm not making any promises about the cancer, mind. So long as that's understood and you don't nag me."

"I'll try not to," Cait said, smiling back. "Only I'm not making any promises about not trying to change your mind."

GLASS HOUSES

*"We are all strangers in a strange land,
longing for home, but not quite knowing
what or where home is."*
MADELEINE L'ENGLE

❧

T HE SECOND OF THE SHORTBREAD CHRISTMAS TREES that Cait had fashioned turned out better than she'd hoped, especially given that she'd left the first attempt in the oven long enough that it had baked to a caramelized brown instead of the delicate ivory it was meant to be. She iced the second attempt in a mixture of milk, vanilla, and confectioner's sugar, and then hand-painted green branches, red balls, and gold ribbon by dipping a brush first in whiskey and then in food coloring. If it tasted as good as it looked, she decided as she finished cleaning up and looked down at the finished effort, she could do variations of this for the Tea Room. Offering five or six different types of painted shortbread, a mixture of pastries from the hotel, her mum's famous scones, and a variety of soups and tea sandwiches, she thought she could make the menu work.

She hoped.

Working quickly because she was running out of time, she wrapped the tree as a gift for Brice and set it on top of the fish she had already sealed up earlier in a plastic bin. The sound of the shower upstairs had finally stopped, so she decided her father was done, and she galloped up to shower herself and dress in a red hip-length sweater and a nice black skirt over tights and black suede boots.

She was glad she'd taken the trouble when Brice arrived. His hair was still damp, and he'd put on clean gray trousers, a pale blue shirt, and a soft sweater beneath his leather jacket. He looked wonderful, but it struck her abruptly that he, too, looked tired. Which was no wonder considering the time he'd been putting in for her at the Tea Room in addition to whatever other work he had going at the garage.

He helped her father into the back seat of the Land Rover, then came around to open the door for Cait, surprising her yet again. The way he smiled at her warmed her cheeks, and she slid in quickly and busied herself with the seat belt while she held the warm plastic container with the fish on her lap.

Her nerves grew as they approached the small cottage where he lived. She hadn't seen it since the day she'd left the glen, and she didn't know how she was going to feel. Whether she had really let all the old hurt and raw emotion go.

But nothing looked the same as Brice turned into the drive that led to the garage and his cottage. The old garage building that she remembered—half-derelict with a leaky roof, a broken window, and only a single bay for car repairs—had been fixed and painted. Beside it, an entirely new building had been added with three additional bays hidden behind automatic doors. Above that, higher on the hillside, the small structure where Brice had been raised had grown into a fair-sized house, with additional rooms added onto the original building and a whole new second level added on as well. Surrounded by decking that appeared to circle the building on both levels, floor to ceiling picture windows looked down over the treetops to the loch. The moon was out, just shy of full, and it reflected brightly off the glass, combining with lights that blazed inside to make the entire structure sparkle. The whole house looked as though it had been made for the landscape, grown out of it, with naturally wood-stained walls and all those windows to reveal the view.

Brice mashed a garage door clicker and pulled into a pristinely white-painted space alongside the house, then he switched the Land Rover's engine off.

Cait turned in her seat to face him, feeling shocked. And more than a little stupid. "Did you build all this?"

"Not all of it. I had help putting up the framework and then paid to have the difficult bits done. The plumbing and electrical, and the fireplace, roof, and windows. I've had a few of the lads in at weekends helping, too."

"Why didn't anyone tell me?" Cait asked, feeling as though she'd been asking that question far too often lately. Feeling wrong-footed all too often.

"Where'd the money come from?" her father demanded from the back seat. "That's the bigger question."

"Nothing illegal." Brice sounded even more tired—and . . . disappointed. Definitely disappointed.

Had he imagined this moment, Cait wondered, envisioned showing her what he had built? That had to be part of inviting the two of them here. Had he been hoping for her approval? For her father's?

But how *had* he done this? And where had the money come from? And why? *Why* build all this?

He came around to meet her as she slipped out of

the car. Taking her hand, he pulled her toward a side door that led inside. "Do you like it?"

She paused in the doorway, stunned.

The balconies around the house had no railings, the inside wasn't quite finished yet, and there wasn't much in the way of furniture, but the bones of the place were . . . perfect. She couldn't have chosen them better herself. No interior walls divided the space or obstructed the views of the glen. A tidy, modern kitchen on one end flowed into a dining area which became a beautiful, high-ceilinged area that culminated in a fireplace that tapered dramatically into a slate-tiled chimney surrounded by honey-colored walls. Brice's familiar old sofa and two battered armchairs sat in front of it along with a low table and a pair of end tables whose surfaces were marred by a mosaic of stains left by countless beer bottles and whiskey glasses.

She had spent more time than she cared to think curled up with Brice in the chairs, on that sofa, putting her own beer bottles down on torn napkins or dirty dishes so that she didn't contribute to the patchwork of stains on the tables. Maybe that was why the whole house seemed familiar. But Cait didn't honestly believe that. Everything about the house felt as though she knew it. Everywhere she looked, she found something that was exactly as though she had chosen to put it there herself, the color and pattern of the slate around the fireplace, the fact that there was no mantel to clutter the clean look of it, the warm honey of the paint, the dark stained oak on the floor, the windows with that view, the way the staircase up to the second level seemed to hang, suspended by nothing at all, in the air. The balconies. She could picture herself spending hours and hours sitting on those balconies watching the light change on the loch. Watching the sun set and rise again. Watching the seasons change.

"It's still a work in progress," Brice said, his expression still too anxious. "I'll get new furniture for it eventually, and I haven't put in the bookshelves on that back wall there—they'll go from floor to ceiling eventually. And I'm not quite done with two of the bedrooms and the guest bath upstairs."

It was all too much for Cait to take it in. "I can't believe you've done this—all of this."

But that hadn't come out right. It wasn't what she meant to say at all. It sounded too critical, not nearly awed enough by the achievement, and she needed him to see that she understood. Turning, she caught his arm, held him in place until he was forced to look at her instead of trying to study the house with a critical eye as he had been.

"It's absolutely beautiful," she said. "Incredible.

It would be even if you'd spent five years building it. I can't believe you've managed to get so much done since I was here."

"I've Brando to thank for getting me started. He went in with me to buy a Jaguar I restored, and I sold that for a fair bit then reinvested in a McLaren. I delivered an Aston Martin DB5 to a client just this morning, the biggest restoration so far."

"How did you find the time?" Cait asked. "Not to mention the knowledge. You've always been a brilliant mechanic and I mean no disrespect, but don't those cars require specialized technicians and engineers?"

Brice smiled, a wry smile, not a happy one. "I find cars with problems I can manage, and I hire specialists when I need them. I've learned a lot and done a few certifications. The truth is, without you here, there hasn't been a whole lot I wanted to spend time doing. Mostly, I work. Either here at the garage or on the house."

"But why?" Cait couldn't help asking, couldn't help feeling like she needed to hold her breath. "Why push yourself so hard to do all this?"

He leaned in closer and said into her ear, "Because every day when I woke up I discovered all over again that you weren't here, and every night when I went to bed, I dreamed that in the morning you'd be back. I hoped you would finally realize that this place, with me, is where you are meant to stay. I needed to believe that."

SHARDS

*"Love never dies a natural death.
It dies because we don't know
how to replenish its source."*

ANAÏS NIN

C AIT FINISHED WASHING THE LAST of the colored earthenware dishes and handed it to Brice for drying. It was a new set, one she had never seen before, but she liked the simplicity of it, each plate a different primary color without any pattern or artifice that had made a beautiful backdrop for the beef roast, Yorkshire pudding, and roasted vegetables that Brice had served. Picking up her half-empty wine glass, she watched him stack the plates and tuck them away inside a cabinet. He'd taken off his sweater and rolled up the sleeves of his pale blue shirt, and his skin looked darker with the contrast, the muscles beneath it lean and hard. Not gym muscles as she'd seen in London. These were the real thing, honed through pure hard work.

She was proud of him. Not because he'd built a house for her, although the thought of that still made it hard to breathe. Because he had somehow come into his own while she'd been gone, figured out who he was so that he now walked comfortably in his skin. Confidence, she decided, could be sold as an aphrodisiac and peddled to the masses. Whoever figured out how to bottle it would make a mint.

"What are you thinking about so intently?" Brice asked, turning back after he'd closed the cabinet door.

Cait took a sip of the wine, a Pinot Noir with a deep, full perfume that made her want to breathe it in. Like Brice himself, it went to her head, made her want to taste, savor, linger.

"I'm wondering where you learned to cook like that," she asked. "You used to stick to bangers and mash."

"I followed the recipes," he said, smiling back at her. "Shock, I know, given that I've never liked instructions much. I just told myself it was chemistry."

"You nearly failed chemistry, if I remember right."

"Did I really?" He folded the dishcloth and came closer to hang it on the rack beside her hip, watching her the entire time.

"Maybe not all chemistry," she admitted.

He laughed and split the last of the wine in the bottle between his glass and hers. With a glance at her father, who was still watching the telly by the lighted fireplace, he put a finger over his lips and pointed toward the sliding glass door that led out onto the balcony. She nodded, and he slipped his sweater back on then helped her into her coat. Once they were outside, he slid the door closed behind them.

"Here, keep hold of my hand and sit right there," he said, motioning to the edge of the decking.

She sat cautiously, legs dangling over the drop, while he settled himself beside her, watching the moon ride high, its reflection nearly round as it reflected on the surface of the loch. The night was as clear as a diamond, cold and crisp. Cait shivered, though not because of the temperature. Between the wine and Brice, she didn't feel chilled at all.

"This seems to be my day for apologies," she said. "I owe you one. You were right about there being more to my leaving than seeing Rhona coming out of your cottage. I've been over and over it in my mind, and I know that I wasn't thinking of leaving when I came over. But I jumped at the chance to get away. I jumped to conclusions, and I should have trusted you. At the very least, I should have talked to you about it instead of writing a note and wrapping it around my ring. I was scared."

"Scared of me?" Brice asked.

"Scared of everything. Scared of myself. Scared the way I hadn't been since you and Brando dared me to climb up the side of the copper still the first time we broke into the old distillery."

"We didn't know Mad Mackenzie was going to come by in the middle of it."

"I never minded the bruises. It was being startled when he shouted, and then the sense of falling and falling and falling as if I'd never stop. Slow motion falling. I walked into your house after seeing Rhona, and I saw the bottle and the empty glasses in the kitchen, and I saw the sheets all tangled on the bed. You were in the shower, and it was as if I was walking from room to room falling and falling, and I felt like if I hadn't left, I would have crashed to the ground."

"I'm sorry. It wasn't—"

"I believe you. I should have believed in you. That's what you told me the other day, and you were right."

"You're here now, though. Aren't you?"

Cait couldn't decide whether he was asking if she

was physically real—or whether he wanted to know if she was back, if *they* were back, the two of them. But a simple "yes" worked fine as an answer either way.

Brice took the glass out of her hand and set it down beside his on the decking, and then he leaned forward and caught her face between his palms. It seemed to take forever for his lips to reach hers, but then they stayed, moving thoroughly and excruciatingly, sweetly, slow. Finally he pulled back.

"Not here," he said, "glass houses and all that." He gestured back to where the blue light of the telly her father was watching flickered through the window. "Anyway, you'll be frozen through soon."

"It's probably time to get Dad home anyway. He'll be due for his dose of pain medication."

"I'll go get the car warmed up."

Cait got her father's cane off the floor by the sofa and handed it to him, then tried to hold his coat for him, but he snatched it out of her hands. "I'm not a bloody invalid."

"You're a bloody something," she said. "I won't say what."

He shot her a look then chuckled. "Your mother used to call me far worse, though not where you or Rob could hear her."

It was the first time since Cait had come home that

he'd referred to her mum as if the memory brought him pleasure instead of pain. Cait squeezed his hand, and he squeezed hers back and, later, as they were all driving back home the short distance up the hill, her in the rear seat and Brice and her father up front beside each other, she allowed herself a dangerous burst of optimistic anticipation not far removed from the kind she used to feel as a child on Christmas night, as if something wonderful was coming and she had only to be patient and let the time tick slowly past. Her father had been perfectly pleasant over dinner, and he'd even complimented Brice on the house and on the meal.

He would find his way back, she was increasingly certain of it. He'd fight, and he would beat the cancer, and she and Brice would finish the Tea Room and get it open, and she and Brice . . . Well . . . Was it stupid to feel certain that would work out, too? She felt no doubts about it, only a dead calm certainty that brought her a sense of peace.

Peace which lasted only until they reached the drive and saw that it was filled with cars.

"What's all this?" her father asked.

Cait recognized Elspeth's car, and Brando's Land Rover, and the Audi that belonged to Connal MacGregor. And through the window, a half dozen heads were visible bobbing around the sitting room.

Her father thumped the dashboard and turned to

look at Cait. "Did you give them permission to be here? In my house! What do they think they're doing?"

"No, *our* house," she said, "and I've absolutely no idea." She climbed out of the Land Rover the moment Brice had pulled it to a stop, and she hurried down the path and threw the front door open. Elspeth and Kirsty Greer met her as she stepped into the hall.

"I'm sorry," Elspeth said, sounding a little out of breath. "We were meant to have been done and gone already, but there was more to do than we'd thought, and I've had trouble remembering where Morag kept everything." Her short graying hair was tied back with a kerchief, and she wore an old fisherman's sweater over jeans that she'd rolled up at the bottom. Added to a smudge of dust on the side of her nose, the outfit made her look entirely unlike herself.

Cait shook her head. "What do you mean where my mother kept things?" she asked as her father and Brice came through the door behind her. "What things?"

But her father pushed past her and continued through into the sitting room and something gave a dull thud and then rolled across the floor with a clatter. Cait hurried after him and came through the doorway to see him stopped dead a few feet into the room, staring at a live Christmas tree that Brando's Emma, Anna MacGregor, and little Moira were busy decorating. Moira held the empty hook of one of the little gold balls that Cait's mother had hand-painted with holly leaves and the ornament itself lay on the wide deep red tree skirt that Cait's grandmother Stewart had hand embroidered, a few feet away where it had rolled when Moira dropped it.

"What the devil d'you think you're doing?" Donald shouted, glaring at Moira and the rest of them. "Who gave you permission to touch any of this?"

Cait ran the few steps to Moira and squeezed her shoulders, letting her know it was all right. "It's fine— clearly they're trying to give us a lovely Christmas," she said. "They're neighbors trying to help."

But it wasn't only the tree that they had come to put up. The emptiness of the sitting room around her was gone as well. The things of her mother's that Brice had carted up to the attic on her father's instructions had all been brought back down again to fill the voids they had left behind: the photographs on the mantel, the painting of Santorini on the wall, the collection of her mother's porcelain figurines, the chess set.

Anna MacGregor, her expression fierce beneath her dark long curls, came and looped her arm through Moira's elbow, glaring at Cait's father like a cat ready to protect her kittens. Moira, wide-eyed, shifted to stand closer beside her, and with Anna there, Cait moved to placate her father instead.

"It all looks wonderful—" she started to say as she approached him, but he rapped the edge of the little table with his cane and then pointed it at her.

"Is this why you wanted me out of the house?" he demanded. "You and Brice and the rest of them cooked this up behind my back?" His face was the sort of mottled red that used to go along with a voice that had seemed, when Cait was younger, loud enough to shake the house. He was a little quieter now, but his anger was just as deep.

"I didn't know. I promise you I didn't," Cait said. She caught his arm, pleading with her eyes. "It's very kind of them to go to all this trouble, though, isn't it? They were all trying to give us a lovely Christmas."

"If I'd wanted any sort of Christmas, I would have done one myself. This isn't kind,"—he looked straight at Elspeth Murray who stood behind him in the doorway—"it's meddling. It's judging. This will be all around the glen by morning, everyone knowing poor, old Donald Fletcher can't bear looking at anything that used to belong to his wife. Well, I won't have it." He let his glare sweep the room, until it fixed on Brice again. "You," he said. "You're the one who put them up to it, didn't you? Did you think this would get you into my good graces? Or is it Cait's blessing you're still after? Should have known you'd never change. You always did have to be the one to win the fight. No matter who got hurt."

Cait grabbed both her father's forearms. "Stop. Stop it now, before you say anything you'll regret."

"Why should I regret a bloody thing?" He wrenched away from her and lost his balance so that he had to take a quick step to keep from stumbling, and the effort only made him angrier still. "My only shame is that I let you come back here again." He poked her in the chest with his index finger. "Let you take up with *him* all over again. Don't you see? It doesn't matter how much money he throws around, how many houses he builds, how many posh meals he serves up. His father was a drunk who used his fists to show everyone how important he thought himself. Brice is no different. He doesn't give a thought to how anyone feels, and when you're with him, you're no better. You used to be a good girl before you met him. Prickly, aye, but helpful, too, and mindful of how you were raised. Now look at you. Well, I'm tired to death of it. Weren't for your mother coddling you, you'd have had to pick sides a long time ago, and I'm telling you right now to make a choice. You want to stay in this house, you stay away from him. If you go, stay gone. You leave this house tonight, you'll never set foot in it again, and that's a promise."

A hot flood of words bottled up inside Cait, ready to throw at him. She wanted to tell him he was wrong, and selfish, and . . . and *mean*. But he stood in front of her, shaking, leaning on his cane with both hands as if he needed them both to keep from collapsing. He wouldn't hear a thing she said to him right now anyway. She knew him too well to believe otherwise, and if she said even a fraction of what she was thinking, he really would kick her out of the house. Then who would be there to look after him?

No one. Apart from Brice, he'd managed to chase the whole village away after he'd broken his ankle, and now they'd come back and he'd done the same and worse.

Turning to Brice and Elspeth, she silently mouthed, "I am so sorry," then she took her father's elbow and steered him toward the stairs. On the upstairs landing, Brando and Angus Greer and Connal MacGregor had come out of Donald's bedroom and stood quietly looking down at the commotion.

Cait mouthed, "I'm sorry," up at them, too.

Her father wrenched away from her and shook his cane at Brando. "What were you doing in there?"

Brando glanced at Brice and ran a hand through

his chin length hair, but it was Connal MacGregor with his jaw set and his famous blue eyes narrowed, who stepped forward and answered him, and it had been MacGregors who'd run the glen long enough that his anger carried weight. "We brought your bed down from the attic and put it back together for you so your daughter could have her own back to sleep on, Donald Fletcher. You surely don't want to see her sleeping on the floor in her own house?"

"She can sleep on any bleeding bed she chooses." Donald made a growling noise in his throat, turned, and limped back into the sitting room. "*I'll* be sleeping on the sofa."

"Enough!" Elspeth stepped in front of him, hands on her hips. "You're a grown man, and your Morag would be shamed the way you're behaving now. Don't you see that? You think there's no one else in the world who's grieving the loss of someone they loved? Regretting mistakes they made? Everyone has regrets. We all go on the best we can. Feeling sorry for yourself and closing the door on the people who care about you, lying to the people who love you, that won't help anything. You can't wall away every trace of your old life and pretend you're still alive. You had us fooled for a while, telling us you were all right, but we're seeing you clearly now. Clearly enough to suggest you need to find a mirror to look into. Do that, take a good, hard look, and ask yourself if you're liking what you see."

Donald had gone still, a little vein throbbing at his temple. Cait barely had time to brace herself for the explosion before it came.

"Get out," he yelled. "Get out, the lot of you! And take all this with you. Take it away!" He swept his cane over the collection of porcelain figurines—the farmer and his wife, the little dancer in green with the red pompom on her cap, the pair of Staffordshire Scottish terriers that Cait and Robbie used to take turns hiding. The pieces crashed to the floor and shattered.

It felt to Cait as though the shards had flown straight into her heart.

She wanted to shake her father, shake some sense into him, but when she turned to him, she stopped.

He was standing there staring at the broken pieces on the floor, breathing hard, his shoulders shaking. She had never once seen him cry, not when the army had come about Robbie, not when he'd held Mum's hand while she took her final breath. He'd spilled his tears in private then, and seeing them slipping quietly down his cheeks now, Cait's anger all seeped away.

She went and put her arms around him. He pushed her aside and limped toward the bathroom with his back stiff and his shoulders still trembling. He didn't quite slam the door, but he came darn close.

When he was gone, there was silence, and no one moved. Cait fought to pull herself together. Clearing her throat, she turned toward the others and spread her hands in a gesture of defeat. "I'm sorry. I know you meant this kindly," she said, looking around at all their familiar faces, touched by what they'd done but also furious because their timing could not possibly have been worse. "He's having a hard time with all he's been through—"

Connal MacGregor moved down the stairs, his smile a little wry. "The more men know they're behaving like idiots, the more they'll fight to the teeth to defend what they're doing. There's not one of us who hasn't been in the same place as your father, one way or another. With less excuse than he has, come to that. No need to apologize for him."

His eyes met Anna's above Cait's head, and they softened immediately. Anna came and gently touched Cait's shoulder. "I never got to meet your mother," she said. "She was too sick by the time I came to the glen, but I've heard about how much she did for everyone."

Kirsty moved closer, too, absently rubbing the sweet, enormous arc of her pregnancy bump. "Aye, and we're not here for Donald Fletcher. We're here for Morag's sake, and yours. To repay a fraction of what your mum did for all of us. I used to live for the books I got from the library—and she always made sure she had something new for me. She knew what I was going to love, and setting books aside for me the way she did, it made me feel special, as if there was someone who understood me. My mum's been telling everyone about the photos she brought you to hang up in the Tea Room. All her friends are talking about the old stories they've given you. But the rest of us, the younger ones, we don't have any of that. All we can offer is support and elbow grease, and if it means that you will keep the Library and Tea Room open, we'll all of us do anything we can to help. I'll need to take a bit of time off with the babe, but I'd love to come back to work when I can. And I know Mairi and the others would, too, so long as your father's not there making everybody feel they can't do anything right."

"That would be wonderful," Cait said, the words feeling heavy and damp and as though they came straight from her heart.

Down the corridor, the bathroom door creaked open, and her father's heavy halting footsteps alternated with the thump of the cane on the old oak floor. Unwilling to spoil the effect of Kirsty's goodwill with another tirade from her father, Cait made a shooing motion with her hands and the others nodded at each other, gathered their coats, and moved to make a hasty exit.

FALLING

"Sometimes good things fall apart
so better things can fall together."
MARILYN MONROE

G UILT GNAWED AT BRICE while he drove home, and though he would have loved to put the blame somewhere else, he couldn't deny it fell squarely on his shoulders. He should have known that having Brando and the others bring Morag's things from the attic wasn't a good idea. His mind had been on Cait, hoping to make her happy. Somehow, he'd forgotten that right now making her father happy and healthy was Cait's first priority. The sad truth was, with the way Donald carried on, it had been easy to focus on what seemed to be overreaction and lose sight of the very real fact of his illness. Brice wouldn't make that mistake again.

He parked in the garage beside the house and stayed in the car to dial Cait's number. It rang and rang and eventually went to voice mail. He could picture her trying to wrestle Donald to bed, or worse, sitting there with him, watching him cry. But knowing her father, crying had likely gone back to shouting. Brice hated not knowing. Rubbing the back of his neck, he left a message for her and disconnected, then went back into his house.

The place seemed colder without Cait.

He'd liked having her here. Talking to her, doing dishes together. They'd made progress. Come so close to fixing things between them.

He tried the phone again, but there was still no answer.

Christ, he needed a drink. In the kitchen, he pulled a bottle of Scotch from the cupboard and started to reach for a glass. But Cait had left the kitchen spotless and he found himself reluctant to change a single thing about the way the house looked since she'd gone, as if not changing it would make it easier for her to step back inside. Which, he thought as he unscrewed the cap on the bottle and took a swig, was an entirely ridiculous notion.

The warmth of the whiskey slid pleasantly down his throat and started to fill the sunken, worried emptiness in his gut. Carrying the bottle with him, he walked through the house with the ghost of Cait's presence keeping pace beside him. He stood by the fireplace where the coals of the fire he'd laid after dinner still glowed orange.

Thinking about the evening, thinking about her and her father, not knowing what to do for either of them, the helplessness of it all got to him. The certainty that she was in pain tonight, and he couldn't be there for her, left him feeling as though someone had sliced away his skin and left the nerves exposed.

He wasn't good at feeling helpless. He'd spent too much of his childhood with impotent fury tearing at him. There were too many people in the world who smelled the faintest whiff of weakness and honed in on it, twisted it, for their own pleasure. His father'd been one of them, and years before he'd gone and gotten himself killed in a bar fight in Glasgow, Brice had learned to armor himself in anger and attitude and never let his own weakness to be used against him.

For Cait, he'd lay himself bare. Take any blow.

The pain on her face when she'd seen her father crying, though, that was down to Brice's own carelessness. He'd caused that. The fact that his intentions had been good didn't matter. He was the one who had given the key to Brando. He'd seen for himself that Cait was bringing Donald around, inch by inch, but he'd risked spoiling it by pushing too hard and backing Donald into a corner where he had to face everything he'd been avoiding all at once.

Who knew what Donald was thinking now? What he was saying to Cait?

And Cait wasn't the forgiving sort. Never had been.

Brice looked around the house, and her ghost was suddenly everywhere. Washing dishes in the kitchen, laughing as she found the coin he'd carefully wedged beneath the marzipan icing in Emma's fancy Christmas cake. Cait's wineglass stood on the table beside the sofa when she'd set it down to pick up her father's cane from the floor and folded the blanket she'd draped over him while he was watching the telly. There was a trace of her lipstick along the rim of the glass, a perfect imprint.

Brice tried her number again. Left another message.

Turning his back on the emptiness of the rooms where she'd been, he went upstairs to his equally empty bedroom. He wasn't tired, but he had no desire to go to the pub, or to watch television. If he tried to read, he'd only end up with his mind wandering after every paragraph. He emptied his pockets out onto the dresser as usual, but as he set his wallet down, he stopped and opened it to retrieve the engagement ring he'd been carrying with him since she'd left it with the note inside his mailbox. He'd hoped to give it back to her when the time was right, but now he wondered if they'd ever get there. Whether her father would ever let them get there.

If Donald Fletcher refused to go through with the surgery, he'd have months, maybe years of dying hanging over him. Or years of living, if he decided to have the treatment. Either way, Cait would always be aware that he was on borrowed time.

Brice didn't know what was worse, the idea of making Cait sneak around with him like the worst periods of their teenage years, or making her defy her father openly. In which case, Donald might try to make Cait leave the glen altogether to keep them apart. Cait had always wanted so much to please her father, to have him accept her as she was.

He picked the phone up off the dresser and tried her number again with no more luck than before, then he set the phone down and pulled on a thicker sweater. Taking the Scotch with him again, knowing it was a crutch and not, for the moment, giving a damn, he wandered toward the wall of windows and stood looking out. The angle was wrong, though. Looking uphill toward Cait's house, the view was blocked by trees. He slid open the door to the balcony and walked out to the corner where the angle was better.

Her house blazed with light, upstairs as well as down. Even the dormer window in the attic was lit. Maybe she was up there, putting away all the things that Brando and the others had taken down that evening.

It killed Brice to think of her having to do that by herself. Having to do it at all.

He breathed in a calming lungful of crisp, night air. Listened to the soothing quiet of the glen, the slow shush of melting snow dropping from a tree limb, the chitter of a night bird in the distance. Below him, a wood mouse scurried across the snow, and a tawny owl burst from a nearby hemlock tree and swooped down only a foot or two from Brice in a blur of mottled feathers.

Brice flinched back, startled, but the step took him off the corner of the deck, and suddenly there was nothing at all beneath him.

MOMENTS

*"What matters in life is not
what happens to you
but what you remember
and how you remember it."*

GABRIEL GARCÍA MÁRQUEZ

C ALMING CAIT'S FATHER DOWN involved a glass
of Scotch and a bit of patience finding something
soothing on the telly—something that he'd seen
enough times already that he could easily let himself
drift off to sleep before it was over. Not that she was
anywhere near done with him yet. He wasn't going to
get out of a tongue lashing quite so easily.

She put in a DVD of *Monarch of the Glen* for him
to watch, then sat down beside him on the sofa as the
credits rolled. "Is this what you were like when people
tried to help you after I left?" she asked. "If so, it's a

wonder you've any friends left at all."

"Don't need friends," he said, leaning back against the cushion with his long arms crossed over his stomach.

"You can tell yourself that all you like, but everyone needs friends. If you cut yourself off from human contact, it's no wonder you don't think life's worth living."

He leaned forward and fumbled for his cane. "Can't you let me sit here in peace for one bloody minute? Especially since you don't know what you're talking about."

Cait put her hand on the cane to stop him trying to get up and walk away. "Then tell me. Talk to me. You can't push the memories of Mum out of your life. It isn't healthy, and why would you want to anyway? You had a wonderful life together."

"She would have had a wonderful life with anyone," her father said, trying to wrestle the cane away from her. "She should have had a better life than the one I gave her."

Cait went still. "Is that what this is about? And you think breaking the things she loved is going to fix that or make you remember her life any differently?"

"I don't want to remember it at all!" His voice was filled with such an ache of regret that Cait didn't know how to reach him.

It stung, too, this stubborn insistence that he wanted to forget, because she herself was part of the life he was trying so hard to leave behind. Her and Robbie.

"Is that why you didn't want me to come home?" she asked. "Do I remind you of things you'd rather forget?"

He stopped fumbling with the cane. "Of course you remind me of her." His Adam's apple bobbed as he swallowed hard. "More and more every day, you shame me the same way she did, showing me the things I'm not strong enough to change about myself. Pride, Caitie. It's a powerful thing, and a hurtful one."

"The fact you're seeing it means you're strong enough to change it."

His knuckles went white against the dark glossed wood. "Change takes more energy than I've got left."

"I'm not leaving again," she said very quietly. "I'm going to make the Tea Room a tribute to Mum and all the women of the glen. I told you that already, and I'm not planning to change my mind."

"Aye, you told me. I heard you."

"Well, just so you know."

Headlights flashed by on the road, and Cait wondered briefly if everyone who'd been over had gotten back to their own homes already, their own

Christmas Eve's spoiled after they'd tried to be so kind. She'd need to make up a plate of cookies or something to take around on Boxing Day with apologies.

"I was a coward myself, running off to London. I see that now," she said. "There were things here I needed to resolve, but I couldn't bear to stay and face them. The problem is that we can't outrun the things inside ourselves. You can't hide them away forever in the attic, either. You break them and you break away pieces of yourself."

He wrenched the cane away when she wasn't expecting it and stood up. Looking down at her in the dim light, in that moment he was as large and terrifyingly stern as he used to seem when she was little. Then she saw that he was shaking, and the impression faded.

"I'm already broken," he said.

"You don't have to be." Cait stood up beside him. "And I've no intention of putting Mum's things away."

"I'll do it myself, then. If you won't."

She put a hand on his arm, her face turned up to his with all the hurt and hope that was inside her laid bare. She'd tried anger, and defiance, and recklessness, and none of those had ever worked on him at all, so she had to be smart enough to try something else.

"I remember you telling Robbie that cowardice is the saddest type of human failing," she said. "Do you remember that?" She pointed to a spot by the doorway. "He stood right there in his brand-new uniform with his duffel bag across his shoulder, and you told him he was a coward, turning his back on his obligations, on his family."

"Aye, I told Robbie that, and he set out to prove I was wrong and got himself killed for his trouble." Her father's words came out raw, as though each one was ripped from his heart.

Cait's chest squeezed in sympathy and tears suddenly filled her eyes. Her own throat ached. "Is that what you think? That Robbie was trying to prove his courage? You knew him better than that. Robbie would have done anything in the world for someone he loved. Given anything. That was who he was, who Mum—and you—raised him to be. You taught him that the Fletcher name was something to be honored, but Mum taught him to honor life. You know him better than to think for a moment that he would throw himself away for the sake of honor or courage or anything abstract. It was people who mattered to him. He would never have regretted giving his own life up to save someone else."

"I can regret it for him. But maybe I am a coward, if that's the point you're making. They say you hate in others what you see inside yourself." He stumbled toward the bathroom, and as he reached the door he said. "If you want to keep your mum's things out, keep them. I won't sleep in the bedroom with them, though. I'll stay down here on the sofa."

Cait couldn't help feeling that if she'd won a victory at all, it was small and hollow. She brought down her father's pillow and sheets and quilt from the bedroom and made the sofa up for him as best she could. She brought down his pajamas, too, and over his objections, helped him take the walking cast off his ankle. Only once she had him settled and watching the last of the *Monarch of the Glen* episode did she quietly sweep up the shards of porcelain from the floor while he deliberately looked the other way.

Back in the kitchen, she emptied the dustpan into the bin and brewed herself a cup of tea. While it steeped she rearranged the few things that Elspeth and the others had put back not quite where they belonged. The Royal Crown Derby salt and pepper shakers belonged on the counter by the stove, and the red and white checkered calendar frame had hung above the photographs on the bookshelf. She would need to buy new pages for it soon. The cookbooks had always been in order from largest to smallest, held in place by the Staffordshire poodle bookends that her mother had claimed looked more like sheep than dogs. Finally, Cait put the book of Stewart family recipes in pride of place back where it belonged. Where it would stay.

The progress she and her father had made was small, but at least he was talking to her. Being honest with her. And she had Brice to thank for it. The thought stirred up a warm glow inside her.

He was more dangerous now than he'd ever been. And she didn't even mind.

It was nearly midnight. Christmas. Walking to the kitchen door, she watched her own reflection getting closer, and she realized that in spite of the upset with her father, despite the chaos and his outburst, despite the way his admission had made her ache for him, she looked almost . . . content. Hopeful.

If only there was a way she could tip the scales and make him see that there was still plenty to live for, and that his guilt over Mum and Robbie was needless. The problem was, like the doctor had said, it was hard to calculate the quality of a life. Neither Mum nor Robbie had lived nearly long enough, Robbie especially, but they had measured their lives in smiles.

Those were the memories that Cait wished her father could remember. All those smiles that added up to a joyous life.

But why couldn't she give that to him?

Here he'd been telling himself that Mum had somehow missed out on something by marrying him and staying in the glen, when the proof of her happiness was tucked away in the attic with all the photographs. Cait had an empty tree to decorate, didn't she? Photographs could make the perfect ornaments.

Tip-toeing up the stairs so she wouldn't wake her father, she climbed up to the attic and sorted through the old albums and loose photos looking for the individual moments that would tell the story of her mother's happy life—a happy life that had included Robbie and made him the kind of man who could become a hero in a country far from the glen. There were so many of them: the one of Mum looking down at a newborn Robbie and Robbie looking back; Cait in her pink newborn hat with Robbie holding her and Mum hovering, smiling from ear to ear; Mum pulling Cait and Robbie on the red toboggan across the frozen loch; Mum laughing as she hung the new yellow curtains in Cait's room the summer six-year-old Cait had decided she hated anything pink; Mum and Cait years later, repainting the front of the Library and Tea Room in an even bolder pink than the one that had been there before; Mum standing by her old Nissan unloading a new (to the library at least) box of books she'd found to stock the shelves.

These and others like them were the memories that her father needed to see so he could finally remember that Morag Fletcher wouldn't have wanted any other life than the one she'd had.

Descending the stairs with a box full of photos to go through and copy and miniaturize, Cait stopped in the doorway of the sitting room to make sure her father was still asleep. He was snoring faintly, and he'd dislodged the blanket from his feet. One of his socks badly needed mending—his big toe peeped out like a bald and ugly newborn swaddled in black cloth. He looked so frail lying there, frail and alone, but he still had her. Family was what Christmas was for, arguments and gifts and memories that all had meaning only because there was so much history and love behind them.

Cait set the box down and covered him with the blanket. Then she retrieved her purse from where she'd left it on the floor in all the fuss, and when she checked her phone she discovered that Brice had left her seven different messages. She'd switched it to vibrate earlier, so she hadn't heard it ring, and now she dumped the purse on top of the box and rang him straight back even as she walked toward the kitchen.

It was already very late. So late that, twining

around Cait's legs, Mrs. Bogan did her best to pretend that it was time for breakfast, and when Cait didn't immediately stoop to pick her up, she went to her bowl and sat beside it, black-tipped tail nicely wrapped around her paws and her blue eyes so intent on Cait that they appeared even more crossed than ever.

"It isn't nice to beg," Cait said to her while the phone rang and rang and rang. "You've already had all the food I'm going to give you, and I have enough guilt in my life already without you trying to add to it."

Mrs. Bogan threw herself onto her belly beside the bowl as if her strength had given out.

"Drama queen," Cait said.

Brice still hadn't picked up, but when the call went to voicemail, she disconnected and rang him back again instead. There was still no answer.

And suddenly, Cait thought back to the way he and the others had left, to what her father had said. To all the things she *hadn't* said to defend Brice, though now she wished she had.

She mashed the play button on the first of his voicemails. "Cait? I'm so sorry about that. Brando and I were only thinking you deserved to have a Christmas. We—I—didn't mean to hurt your father's pride and make things worse. Call me back, would you? We can figure a way to fix this."

The second message was essentially the same, but by the third he was getting anxious. "Please call me back, Cait. At least to let me know you're all right. I'll come and work it out with your dad tomorrow somehow, only don't shut me out again."

The seventh message was the worst of the lot. "All right, if you don't want to talk to me, I understand. I've made a mess of everything again. I usually manage to, somehow. I want you to know, though, that I am not my father. Just as you aren't yours. I know you're likely thinking he's the only family you have now, but he isn't. You are all the family I have ever needed, and I will always be here for you. Right here. Waiting."

The warm shimmer of feeling she'd had earlier swelled into an emotion too big for Cait's heart to contain. She tried his number again, and when he still didn't answer, she left a message. "I'm *not* not talking to you, Brice. Far from it. If you were here, I'd kiss you for all you've done and tried to do, and I'm an idiot. I've been an idiot. Call me back."

She hung up and tried not to be impatient for the phone to ring. In the meantime, she made up a quick batch of salt dough, cut it into frames of various shapes, and pressed pretty snowflake designs into the surface of them using one of her mum's old lace doilies she'd found in the back of a trunk upstairs. When she'd slid the two cookie sheets full of frames into the oven, she dialed Brice again. But there was still no answer.

The warm glow inside her had started to fade by then, replaced with a niggling worry that something wasn't right. Brice never went far from his phone, and he slept with it beside his bed. Even if he'd been in the shower the first time she had rung, he would have been out by now. Duncan and Flora always closed the pub early on Christmas Eve, so he couldn't have been there, either, and there weren't many other places where he wouldn't have heard the phone ring.

She picked through a few more photographs distractedly and set them in a stack to scan and print in sizes small enough to fit the frames that she had made, but she found herself less and less able to concentrate. She put the stack aside and went to retrieve her keys and coat. Ignoring Mrs. Bogan's inquiring meow, she ran out to her car and headed down toward Brice's house.

FEAR

"Do not be afraid; our fate
Cannot be taken from us; it is a gift."
DANTE ALIGHIERI
INFERNO

L IGHTS STILL FLOODED BRICE'S HOUSE both on the
ground floor and upstairs when Cait arrived, but
the door was locked and no one answered when she
rang the bell. His Land Rover was in the garage; she
discovered that much by climbing up on the hood of
her own car and peering through the small windows at
the top of the automatic doors.

Shivering from more than the cold wind that blew
flurries of snow from the surrounding trees, she tried
to think what to do. She rang his phone again, then
searched the online directory for a land line. All she
found was the garage number and a listing for

MacLaren of Balwhither—Sports Car Restoration. The garage had been dark as she passed it, but she tried both numbers anyway without success. Then she stepped back from the house as far as necessary to peer through the lighted windows deep into the upper floor. There was a sitting area along the front, and a small empty room, but no bedrooms were visible. Needing to see deeper into the house, she gathered her coat closer and stomped through the few inches of snow around the side of the garage.

Lights blazed on that side of the house as well, though the ground itself was shaded by the decking and lit only by the moon shining between the trees. Cait moved carefully, picking her way around brush and rocks and what she suspected were the foundations of future flowerbeds. Then the moonlight glittered on a bit of broken glass in snow that smelled of whiskey. That smell was odd, but she didn't have time to dwell on it. Beyond the broken glass lay a darker form, man-shaped. Unmoving.

Fear knifed through her, skewering her in place like a cold steel blade at the same moment instinct told her to rush forward. Still uncertain what she was seeing, she made herself move cautiously, her heart thudding, wanting—needing—to find herself mistaken. But she recognized the curve of Brice's back, the nape of his neck that stood out taut as a bow as he lay on his side curled in around himself.

"Brice?" she called, moving closer. Her voice was thin with fear, so she tried again. "Brice?"

He didn't answer.

The snow around him had been disturbed, she noted that, as if he had floundered around and dragged himself some distance. There were no footsteps, not from the area that lay beyond him. She looked back the way she'd walked and saw only her own coming from that direction. Only then did she look up, and she saw the sliding glass door standing open on the upper level, the lack of railings around the balconies.

She had her phone out dialing 999 before she'd even moved to kneel beside him, but though she longed to touch him, to shake him, she refrained as she gave the dispatcher the location and information. The rise and fall of his chest and the small clouds of breath from his nose told her he was alive. That was all that mattered.

She hadn't known how much it mattered until this very moment.

Holding the phone against her shoulder, she brushed his hair out of his face and watched him breathing as she talked, willing him to breathe. She pulled his hands out of the snow and tried to warm them, wishing she dared to lift his head and put her coat beneath it.

He groaned as she rubbed his hands, and her heart thudded. She leaned forward, dropping the phone into the snow. "Brice?"

He groaned again. His eyes opened. Blinked. Focused on her. "Cait? You came. Oh, Christ, it feels like I was hit by a truck."

"You fell. Do you remember? Do you know where you are?"

He tried to lift his head.

"Shh, careful. They're sending the air ambulance. Don't move until it gets here."

"It's bloody cold."

"Does your neck hurt?"

"Everything hurts," he said, and he started to roll over onto his back and gave a grunt of pain, grimacing. "I wasn't drunk. It was an owl going after the wood mouse. It surprised me. You have to know that, Cait. I was drinking but I wasn't drunk."

"Shh," she said again. "It doesn't matter." She shrugged out of her coat and lay it behind his head so that if he did roll over again, he would have it as a pillow, but still she said, "Don't move. You could hurt yourself even more."

Of course he didn't listen. He rolled, and her coat was there, and she was momentarily relieved by both those things, by the fact that he was still doing just as he pleased, until she saw the bruising on the side of his head that had already begun to take on the colors of the purple darkness and the deep blue shadows of the night around them. Beneath his sweater, his shoulder was misshapen, too, most probably dislocated, and his left ankle was contorted. God only knew what else.

It was only then that Cait remembered her phone. Her hands shook as she groped for it in the snow, afraid the dispatcher would have hung up or that they'd been disconnected, but the man was still there, and she told him what she knew, and he promised her help would be there shortly. She put the call on speaker and went back to trying to warm Brice's hands, trying to keep his eyes from closing again, keeping him talking until the banana yellow air ambulance finally landed on the widest part of the drive and the crew came running with a stretcher.

They worked quickly, white helmets and reflective strips on their red suits gleaming in the portable lights while they started an IV and gave him morphine for the pain and immobilized his ankle and shoulder and put a collar on his neck before moving him onto the stretcher for transport.

"Can I go with him?" she asked, her eyes pleading. "I need to go with him."

One of the crew nodded, and she held Brice's hand as they lifted him, refusing to let go. She couldn't let him go alone.

The helicopter had made an uproar landing, the sound of the great blades whoop-whoop-whooping unusual and distinctive enough that all over the village lights flicked on and people emerged in coats and snow boots pulled hastily over their pajamas, blowing on their hands as they hurried over.

Cait remembered the oven when she was duck walking beneath the slowly turning blades of the helicopter's rotors. She turned and searched for a face she could trust in the crowd, and she found herself spoiled for choice. It hit her at that moment that there wasn't anyone in the village who wouldn't help, who wouldn't do anything they could. That all you had to do was meet them part way and they folded you within the community so that in Balwhither you were never on your own, unless you chose to be.

Angus Greer stood closest, so she shouted at him, "I left the oven turned on at my house. Could you go and turn it off?"

"The oven?" he shouted back, cupping his ear.

"Yes, the oven. In the kitchen!" She exaggerated the words as best she could. "And could you find someone to stay with my father in case he wakes up?"

"I don't imagine he's asleep anymore," Angus

yelled.

And that was precisely how Cait felt herself, she realized, as though she'd been asleep for a long time and was only now coming fully awake. Realizing what she'd been missing.

This feeling inside her at the thought of losing Brice was why her father didn't want to keep living without her mother. The idea of a world without Brice in it was unthinkable, the way that life couldn't exist without water or food or oxygen. Maybe love was as essential as any of those other things. Maybe humans were built to need something more than themselves, at the risk of having something inside them wither and became petty and selfish and *wrong*.

But there was a difference between love for other people and being immersed in love with the one particular person who opened your heart wide and made it larger, but also made it vulnerable. Having given her heart to Brice, Cait realized in that moment that she was never going to have it back again.

She had loved him for most of her life, but somewhere along the line she had fallen in love with him in a single heartbeat, so quickly that she couldn't name the moment or the reason. Thinking of all the old doubts, the old fears, she realized that not one of them mattered.

She'd been twelve when she had announced to Robbie that she meant to marry Brice one day.

"In the ruins of the old kirk," she'd said, "while the heather's in full bloom. I'll wear black boots and a long white dress, and Brice will love me and think I'm the most beautiful girl in the world."

Robbie had laughed and ruffled her hair. "The undeniable fact that you're the most beautiful girl in the world won't change regardless of what Brice MacLaren thinks, so don't go getting daft ideas of weddings in your head."

Cait didn't care about weddings, or dresses, or heather. All that mattered was that she couldn't lose Brice.

And she climbed into the helicopter more afraid than she'd been in all her life.

PROMISES

"I don't ask you to love me
always like this,
but I ask you to remember."

F. SCOTT FITZGERALD
MAGNETISM

T HEY KEPT BRICE IN THE HOSPITAL after an
alphabet soup of tests that included x-rays and
CT-scans and MRIs followed by a long delay and
surgery, but thanks to the snow and an innate sense of
self-preservation that had sent him rolling as he hit the
ground, he'd only broken the ankle and both bones in
his lower leg. The damage could have been much
worse.

"If you wanted out of Christmas dinner," Cait
said, when she was finally alone with him beside his
bed, "there were easier ways to do it."

"Aye, well, after what happened, I didn't know if

you were still speaking to me, much less planning to cook for me." He looked pale beneath his weathered tan, and a growth of stubble softened the sharp line of his jaw. The swelling at his temple had darkened to a violent purple and black streaked with angry red, and the color had begun to seep down beneath his eye. Normally full of restless energy, he lay ominously still, his muscles lax and his pupils retracted to pinpricks by the morphine.

Cait reached for his hand. "You had me worried."

"I had me worried, too, for a while—until you came along. Why did you, by the way? It was the middle of the night."

"Guilt, probably. I'd missed your calls, then you didn't answer when I rang. I couldn't think where you could be where you wouldn't hear the phone. The messages you'd left made it clear you weren't likely to ignore me calling."

"Why feel guilty, then? I'm the one who—"

"Stop. It doesn't matter. Nothing matters. They're all old wounds, already mended." Cait leaned forward and kissed him on the forehead.

He pulled her lower, tipped his chin, and kissed her lips. She felt him smile as she sighed and eased away, and he laced his fingers with hers. His hands were more calloused than she remembered them, cracked with hard work and freezing weather. There was lotion in the bathroom, and because she was restless, too, she retrieved it and rubbed it into his skin.

"I could get used to having you spoil me," he said. "Only I'd planned it the other way around."

"Oh, you had plans, did you?" Cait found herself smiling wide again. She couldn't seem to stop smiling now that he was out of danger.

His own smile slipped away, and his eyes darkened. He reached for her hand once more, his grip almost too tight.

"I had *hopes*," he said. "That's why I built the house. Every board I put in place, every nail, every screw, every stroke of a paintbrush was a labor of hope. And I've a confession to make."

Cait's heart gave a dull thud, because she was done with apologies and recriminations. "You don't owe me any more explanations. We've both made mistakes, and we're both going to make more mistakes. That's who we both are, and it's fine. You managed to have enough faith to keep hoping, and now all we have to do is keep moving forward. I want to grow old with you and still be making mistakes."

"That's what I'm trying to tell you. I went down to the loch at Beltane, *mo chridhe*. When you left and wouldn't call back, I felt like the color had gone out of the world. I even drove down to London to look for you once—without an address, because your father wouldn't give me one. I was down at the Inn having a drink, and the laughter and conversation all rang hollow. I walked outside, and the whole glen felt empty without you, so I climbed in the car and headed south. It was stupid. The odds of finding you had to have been ridiculous, but by the time I got there it was coming on noon Sunday, so I spent two hours loitering through Waterstone's in Piccadilly in case you happened by. Then I asked someone for the best independent bookshop in London, and I spent another hour there until I decided you might be too poor just starting out to afford new books, so I went to the Oxfam Bookshop instead. I kept thinking how much you and your mum would have loved it."

Cait's eyes were leaking tears again, but Brice was holding her hand so she couldn't wipe them away. "I have a whole shelf of books in my flat I bought at Oxfam."

"I didn't know where to start with libraries. Most are closed on Sundays anyway, so I wandered aimlessly for an hour, left before dark, and eventually slept at a Services on the M6 feeling stupid. The thing was, I kept feeling as though if the two of us were meant to be, fate should have stepped in and pushed us back together. It's daft, I know, but the idea that you could simply have gone from my life, that was even dafter."

"It was me being stupid," Cait said, "but I needed the time to figure myself out."

"I know. We both did. Only I don't want you to think I didn't ever lose faith. Coming back without having seen you like that, I tried to tell myself it wasn't meant to be. There had never been anything between me and Rhona—I still can't believe you'd think there could have been—but I tried seeing other women after that. None of them were you. By Beltane, I was feeling desperate, so I went down to the loch with everyone else."

She squeezed his hand. "We said we'd never need to do that."

"I needed you. I needed to believe you were coming back."

The legend of the Beltane Sighting had been around for countless centuries, a tradition as woven into the fabric of the glen as the rekindling of the hearth fires at Tom-nan-aigeal or the Hogmanay burning of worries and grudges. There was even a Gaelic poem about the Sighting inscribed on a stone at the tip of the peninsula where the two lochs of the Balwhither glen came together:

On the bright day
in the morning dew
to the pure of heart
the Lake of Destiny
will reveal the true love who
will warm the winter of your life
and the Lake of Enchantment
will turn sight to truth.

Maybe it wasn't only the need for heroes that the Highlands bred, but also the need for something to believe in. Faith in something beyond oneself, beyond the present.

"What did you see?" Cait asked, her chest aching with hope.

"You and me and a son who looked like both of us in a house made of windows that looked out over the lochs and the braes around the glen."

Cait thought of a child that looked like Brice, and she thought of all the things that she would show a child: the waterfall behind the kirk, and the nooks and crannies of the library, the osprey's nest far down the glen, and the wildcat's lair high up Cruach Ardrain where she and her mum had crouched downwind for hours every June, hoping for a glimpse of kittens. They'd seen them only twice, but that hadn't stopped them from going back each year, because seeing a wildcat was a miracle in itself.

Because everyone needed something to look forward to through the long, harsh winter.

"If we're going to have a son," Cait said, "we had better make sure there are good strong railings on the balconies."

"Aye, obviously, I didn't think my timing through enough. I wanted the inside of the house done first."

"If it wasn't for all the extra hardware in your leg now, I'd have said that was a sound enough plan. Good thing there aren't any metal detectors in Balwhither, isn't it? On the positive side, now you and my father can do your physical therapy together."

Brice grinned weakly at the thought of it, then shook his head. "You still think you can talk him into the surgery?"

His words had started to slur with exhaustion, and Cait brought his hand to her lips and kissed each of his fingers in turn. "I'm going to do my best, but I've been wrong all along. He doesn't need memories of the past. What he needs is a reason to look forward instead of back, the promise of something coming. A grandchild would give him that."

"We'd best get to work on it soon, then, you and I," Brice said. "If I close my eyes now, do you promise not to go away? I'm still half afraid that I'm lying in the snow and you're a dream I conjured up out of pain and fear."

"I'm more likely to be a nightmare, but I'll not be going anywhere without you."

Brice closed his eyes, and almost immediately his breathing grew deep and even. His grip on Cait's hand relaxed, and she slowly extricated his fingers from her own. Even without touching him, though, she felt the bonds between them woven so tightly that nothing could be allowed to break them again.

That was the other side of love, a promise that two people made to each other to weather whatever came, day by day and moment by moment. Cait had failed Brice once, but she would never do that again.

SWEETNESS

*"Man prefers to believe
what he prefers to be true."*

FRANCIS BACON

H AVING MISSED CHRISTMAS DAY entirely, Cait decided to combine it with Hogmanay. On the 30th of December, she finished baking a new batch of salt dough frames, painted them gold and silver, then sorted and copied the photographs. Earlier, she'd even managed to find a few games and puzzles and odds and ends at the W.H. Smith's at the hospital in Glasgow. Brice had waited in the Land Rover—which Brando and Emma had been kind enough to bring down for Cait when they'd come to visit at the hospital—once he was discharged so she could run into a Marks and Spencer and buy food and the obligatory sweaters for both him and her father. Now he sat in the sitting room with his leg propped on a pillow after her father had gone up to bed, and he helped her wrap the presents and glue the photographs into the frames.

Cait hung the photos as decorations on the tree along with a few balls and bows and her mother's silver bells. Then she stood back and surveyed her efforts, and tried not to remember that it was the first tree this house had seen since her mum had died.

She refused to think anything but happy thoughts.

"What do you think?" she asked, turning back to Brice. "Will it do?"

His face was an impressive collection of bruises, his right shoulder still in a sling and his right lower leg immobilized in the walking boot. Every movement was agonizing, and even though he hadn't complained, just going up and down the stairs at his house to help her find the things he needed to pack had left him gray with exhaustion. Four days later, and the pain hadn't diminished much.

Still, he managed to smile at her and pat the cushion beside him. "It's beautiful. Now come here."

She went and let him kiss her, briefly, feeling nearly as awkward about it now as she ever had back when they'd stolen kisses in quiet corners of the house, hoping neither her father nor Robbie would catch them. The fact that her father wasn't kicking up more of a fuss about Brice staying here to recuperate—taking over the sitting room, come to that—still surprised her.

Not that she intended to look a gift horse in the proverbial mouth.

She pulled back, then changed her mind and kissed Brice again, simply because she could, because he was still here and she felt the urge to kiss away the tell-tale signs of pain. Catching the spirit of it, he pulled her onto his good knee and kissed her with a thorough, firm, and confident exploration that had every cell in her body humming, aching, wanting more. Her fingers wrapped themselves in the fabric of his shirt, and breathed in the smell of him, the joy of him, savoring the softness of his hair against her cheek, the harshness of the evening stubble on his chin, the warmth of his breath, and the hard, broad muscles that even after all he'd been through held her easily, as though he would never let her go.

Reluctantly, she pulled away. "I still have the Dundee cake to start. Want to come to the kitchen to keep me company?"

He tried to hide it, but she saw the tiny wince of anticipated pain, and she regretted the question immediately. "Aye," he said. "Only give me a minute to get there."

She shook her head. "Why don't you go to bed." She checked her watch, and it was nearly time for his pain medication. "I'll bring you a glass of water so you can take your pill."

He caught her wrist and drew her back. "Cait. I don't want to take any more of those."

"You need them. The doctor said—"

"The doctors can say what they like, but I don't need it."

"A bit of whiskey, then. To help you sleep."

"I don't need that, either."

She looked at him and he looked back steadily, honestly, and she kissed him again, long and hard. Because even though she hadn't asked him for it— would never have asked him for it—he'd just given her a gift she hadn't even known she needed.

She remembered that later as she made the Dundee cake by herself in the quiet kitchen. The familiar motions of the baking made her think of her mother, too, and she could almost pretend that it was still a long-ago Christmas night with the moon playing hide and seek behind billowing clouds that sailed quickly past and left dark moonshadows on the quiet lochs and the village lying tranquil beneath her. Lights shone in windows here and there, the same as they did on Christmas Eve when parents were staying up to manage the behind-the-scenes of Christmas morning, the toys to be assembled, the baking to be done, the last-minute bits of wrapping. Cait's Mum had always worn her Christmas robe after everyone had gone up to bed on Christmas Eve, the terribly ugly green robe that Robbie and Cait had given her as a gift when they'd been too young to realize how hideous it truly was. But it had been the baking of the Dundee cake that had become a private tradition between her and Cait from the Christmas Cait turned nine.

That was the year Mairi MacFarlane had told her there was no Santa Claus.

Not wanting to believe Mairi but at the same time afraid not to believe her, Cait had snuck back downstairs after Mum had put her to bed on Christmas Eve. She'd planned to hide behind the sofa in the sitting room, determined to see for herself who it was that brought the gifts. But it had been Mum who'd caught Cait, and instead of sending her straight back up to bed, she'd let Cait come to the kitchen and help with the cake, creaming the butter and sugar and orange zest and beating in the flour, adding the sultanas, currants, cherries, raisins, and almonds until the dough fairly bristled with them. Whiskey had been the last ingredient, a tablespoon for the cake, one for the cook, and one for Cait, which had finally sent Cait back off to bed with her stomach pleasantly warm and a sense of having done something wonderfully grown up and secret.

That had become a tradition from then on, her and Mum, the two of them making the cake together once everyone else was sleeping. Eventually, Cait had been allowed to do more and more to help, but it had remained the cake that mattered most.

Mum and Robbie'd had their own traditions, too. Traditions that didn't include Cait. Mum had been like that, determined to be fair to everyone and a stickler for precedent. When something wonderful had happened once, it became enshrined forever.

Thinking back on it now, though, Cait couldn't help wondering whether that illicit little bit of whiskey that had made her feel so grown up and secret and pleasantly warm hadn't helped to make it easier to drink with Brice and Brando. Easier to fail to see— until it had all gone a bit too far—that that feeling needed to come from what they did rather than what they drank.

With Brice sleeping downstairs, she went up to bed alone, deeply aware of him a floor below her, also alone. For all the closeness that had developed between them these past days, all the wrongs that had been set right, she couldn't help feeling unsettled. *They* were still unsettled. They'd said all the right things to each other.

Except for one.

She slept fitfully, then got up in the morning still feeling a little groggy. Brice was up already, working on his laptop. "Didn't you sleep?" he asked. "You were up awfully late."

"And you're up terribly early."

He closed the laptop, set it aside, and pulled her closer. "I have a new car to find for a client, and I'll need to hire extra help to get it done. But listen." He picked up a plain manila file that lay on the cushion beside him and held it out to her. "I found this when I needed to use the printer. I couldn't help reading some of the stories you'd transcribed."

Cait took the file and opened it to find the photographs of the women of the glen that she had gathered so far. She had clipped each one to the story she'd been told about the woman in the photo, which she'd carefully typed out and printed.

"Do you know that these stories are wonderful?" Brice asked. "Not just the stories themselves, but the way you've told them? The way you've described the women and how they spoke, the way you've added in the bigger context of how that fits into the history of the glen. It *is* a history of the glen, Cait. A brilliant history, shown from a perspective that no one has ever seen. At least I don't think it's been done."

"That's what I was hoping. Do you think I could write it as a book and sell it?"

"Do I think you could write a book?" Brice's bruised eyes crinkled at the corners as he smiled. "I think you could write a dozen books, but this one isn't just saleable, it's important."

Warmth bloomed in Cait's chest as the acknowledgement settled in. Someone needed to write the stories the women of the glen had entrusted to her. And why couldn't it be her? Not that she had needed Brice's permission, but still, she'd scarcely dared to admit to herself how much she wanted to do this. She'd trained as a journalist. Staying here in the glen didn't mean she couldn't write—it gave her the freedom to write what *she* wanted to explore. If Brice thought the idea was as interesting as she did, maybe other people might think so, too. A history of the Scottish Highlands from the perspective of its female heroes. Its everyday heroes.

"You're wonderful," she said, leaning down to kiss Brice on the lips. "Have I ever told you that?"

"Not often enough," he answered, smiling the smile that crinkled his eyes and burrowed straight into her heart. "Feel free to tell me anytime."

"In that case, I'll tell you again once I've brought you a cup of tea."

By the time she'd brewed a pot and taken it in for him, though, he was deeply immersed on the laptop again. She dropped a kiss on the top of his head and went back to the kitchen, where she softly hummed Christmas carols to herself as she started her belated Christmas morning breakfast.

She was flipping the pancakes on the stove some fifteen minutes later, when the door swung open and her father limped through. Droplets of butter jumped in the pan around the creamy batter, and on the back burner the bacon had begun to sizzle, its aroma an invitation.

Her father stopped and sniffed the air. "Are you cooking what I think you're cooking?"

"I am if you think I'm making Christmas morning pancakes. Since we missed Christmas day altogether, I decided we're going to celebrate today. We'll have Christmas morning, followed by Christmas dinner, and then we'll all go to the bonfire together tonight."

Her father grunted and his lips tightened. "Why would I want to go stand out in the cold for hours on end? I'm too old for all that nonsense."

"You'll go because we're all going," Cait said, glaring at him sternly. "Because it's the end of the year and a chance to put old baggage behind us. Because it's tradition, and I'm asking you to do it. For me."

"Bah!" He grunted again, then braced his cane against the wall and hobbled slowly to the counter where the teapot was still steaming. Watching him, Cait was reminded of what she'd thought each time she'd watched Brice trying to do the simplest task these past few days, each time she'd seen how frustrated his own helplessness made him. It must have been nearly impossible for her father here all alone with his broken ankle.

It was a miracle she hadn't lost him, then. As awful as he'd been to everyone, it was a miracle that Brice had managed to make certain he'd been all right. Which was just one more thing Brice had done for her. One thing among the many.

Leaving the pancakes for a moment, she went to the refrigerator and got the milk out and set it on the counter for her father. But he was staring absently down into his cup.

"Brice is still asleep, I take it?" he asked.

"He's working already."

"He's always working—or asleep," her father said, sounding surly. "I can't even go in there to watch the telly. House is too bloody small for the three of us."

"He's told you it's fine to go in and watch."

"Can't relax with him there, though. Can I?"

Donald shifted and leaned against the counter.

"We can all stay here together, or all go stay at Brice's. One or the other, because I can't be going back and forth all day. And there used to be four of us here."

"That was family."

"You'll need to get used to Brice being family, too."

"Saying so won't make that true." Her father gave her a sharp, hard look. "Anyway, you'll see. The fact he's making an effort now doesn't mean he won't go back to the same lad he always was. But suit yourself if you're determined to throw your life away. I don't need a nursemaid."

"You will once you've had surgery."

"I'll not be letting them cut off my leg!" He set the cup down with a thud. "How many times do I have to tell you?"

Cait smiled to hide the disappointment. "Shame. You'll be missing out, if so."

He gave a suspicious sniff. "Missing out on what?"

"Wait and you might find out," Cait said, though she couldn't help wondering herself how long he would have to wait. Brice had told her about what he'd seen in the loch at Beltane, but that had been the end of the discussion. Maybe she was more old-fashioned than she'd thought, but it turned out there was still at least one topic she didn't feel willing to bring up again herself.

Thinking, these past few days, about what Brice had seen in the loch, she'd had a different perspective as she'd flipped through the photographs she wanted to hang on the tree. She had been so focused on the memories that proved her mum's life hadn't been wasted, it had never occurred to her thinking about how Robbie's death had changed her father. All the things that had ended for him with Robbie gone, and the things he probably thought he would never have again. Someone to carry on his name, his family, his traditions. Someone to whom he could pass along the things his father had passed to him.

He'd always been so proud of Robbie.

She flipped the last of the pancakes out onto the platter and turned off the burner beneath the pan. The bacon was done, too, so she pressed it between a pair of paper towels to mop up the excess grease, and then she used her mother's old trick of sprinkling a dusting of sugar over the top to add a little sweetness.

There was a formula, her mum had always said, to making a man do what needed doing. It involved sweetening him up and greasing the path, and a little sugar on the bacon took care of both.

Cait hadn't had much time to spend with her father these past few days. There'd been too much running back and forth, but she'd been leaving him plenty of food and chores to do here and there as well. As much as he'd grumbled, she could see a change in him already. More color in his face, more energy in his step. Even his eyes were brighter. Now if she could only find a way to broach the subject of the baby again with Brice, if they could find a way to tell her father together, then maybe they could tip the scales for him and finally make him want to fight.

Hoping that wasn't wishful thinking on her part, she set the bacon on a second platter, put both on the table, and pulled the chair out for her father to sit. Then she went out to the sitting room to tell Brice it was time to eat.

GIFTS

"Do not be afraid; our fate
Cannot be taken from us; it is a gift."
DANTE ALIGHIERI
INFERNO

C HRISTMAS DAY AT CAIT'S HOUSE had always
been full of laughter; Brice remembered that.
Aye, Donald Fletcher had glowered and sulked on
every other occasion that he'd been forced to endure
Brice's company, the same as he was glowering and
sulking now, but Morag used to dig her elbow into her
husband's ribs, pop a bit of cake or something sweet
into his mouth, and speak a few words too softly for
anyone else to hear. Though that hadn't improved
Donald's disposition noticeably, it had at least been
enough to keep Donald from booting Brice from the

house.

Brice's own home had never had much in the way of Christmas joy, even before his mother had gone off and left him behind. For a few years after that, Brando's mum had taken him in, but that hadn't been much of a happy house, either. Brando's dad and Brice's father had been cut from the self-same cloth, mean as the devil when they'd been drinking. And for both of them, the time between drinks had shortened year by year. Brando and Brice had run wild together, each of them pretending they didn't mind. Pretending they were stronger than they were. Maybe that's what had made the cow-tipping seem like a lark when Brice had seen it done while he'd been watching the telly one night after his dad had drunk himself to sleep. The ultimate test of strength. Only why tip a cow? That hadn't seemed very sporting to Brice, so he and Brando had snuck into Davy Grigg's pasture in the dead of night and tried to push over Davy's prize Highland bull.

Turned out, bulls didn't sleep so soundly.

And mothers, at least Brando's mum, would defend their children more than they would defend themselves.

Brando'd come home from the hospital with his arm in a cast, and his father had started by adding to the bruises on his face. Brando's mother decided that was the final straw. She put herself between Brando and his father, and it was her own marriage that had broken after that.

Afterwards, the story that Brando's sister Janet tried to put out was that they'd been to Edinburgh to see a marriage counselor. The truth was, driving back in the rain after seeing the solicitor about divorcing, they'd had an accident and both had been killed. Janet, many years older, had stepped in to take care of Brando, but she had blamed Brice for everything that happened. He'd never been welcome in the house again. Had it not been for Cait and her mother, he would have spent every Christmas after that in a cold cottage eating tinned beans and haggis and watching his father drink himself into an early grave.

Spending Christmas Day with the Fletchers had meant more than Brice had ever admitted to anyone. He'd never been there to open presents, though. And he was ashamed to remember how little thought he used to put into the gifts he'd brought for Cait and her family when Morag was kind enough to invite him for dinner.

He intended to change that in the future.

For the moment, though, there wasn't much he could do about presents. Cait had only sprung the idea of celebrating a belated Christmas on him the previous night. Which wasn't to say he hadn't managed to hide a surprise for her beneath the tree, along with the one he'd put together for her and Donald both.

Walking ahead of Brice, Cait swept into the sitting room and took up a position beside the tree while Donald limped in more slowly leaning on his cane. Brice's own progress was even slower. With his arm still in the sling to immobilize his right shoulder, he could only use a crutch on the left arm, which was the opposite of what he needed. It made navigating awkward to say the least.

By the time he reached Cait, she had already started to separate the gifts into piles, and her face was lit with anticipation. That was another thing he loved about her, her moods were as changeable as the clouds that caught themselves on the tops of the high Munros that stood brooding among the smaller Highland braes around the glen.

He settled himself on the end of the sofa where she directed him, while Donald took the other end. She set a stack of gifts in front of him, but he was busy watching for the moment when she would find the two he had hidden himself beneath the tree.

She pulled them out and straightened. "What's this?" she asked, looking at him. "Are these from you?"

"Open the bigger one first," he said, even gladder

now that he had made the effort to rummage in the kitchen for a container large enough to throw her off the scent. In turn, he'd wrapped that with the paper he had hidden beneath the sofa while the two of them were wrapping the other gifts.

Cait studied him a long moment, puzzled. But her eyes gleamed, and he could see she was happy to have something to unwrap. Slowly, she eased the tape off the middle of the package, and then one end and the other. Neatly. Too neatly. He needed to see her reaction when she finally had it open.

But finding a plastic food storage box containing a stack of folded paper towels, her obvious confusion only grew. She pried the lid off, took out the paper towels, and went to set the container down.

"Careful," Brice said.

The ring dropped out onto the floor, bounced once, and then lay on the carpet near her feet.

She stared at it.

Brice picked his crutch up, stood, and came back over to her. "Unfortunately, I can't pick that up for you, and I can't get down on one knee. But I can tell you that when I look back on my life, every good moment has been good because you were there beside me. You make me want to spend every day of the rest of my life finding ways to make you happy. You make me forget myself enough so that I can look around and see the things that are so much more important. You show me how beautiful the world is because you're in it. Marry me, Cait. I don't deserve you, but I swear to you I will spend every minute that I am breathing making sure I never let you down."

Her hand had flown up to cover her mouth, and her eyes had grown full and moist. He'd hoped he knew her answer—dared to hope—but suddenly standing here, his stomach churned and his palms grew slick. What if she wasn't ready for this yet? What if he'd asked too soon? Or used the wrong words?

The doubt started to make him dizzy, but then she stepped forward and kissed him, her lips soft and her thumbs pressing lightly on either side of his mouth. He breathed in the scent of her: warm, spicy Christmas pancakes, honey vanilla shampoo, the new perfume whose name he didn't know but whose scent had become familiar.

"Is that a *yes*?" he breathed against her hair as she drew back.

"Yes, please," she said. "I thought you'd never get around to asking." And turning to her father, she arched her eyebrows and added, "See? Didn't I tell you he was family?"

Donald sat with his arms folded, but not in a

dissatisfied way. More self-protective, Brice decided. Then he wondered, if he ever lost Cait, how he would feel if he saw two lovers happy together. The thought froze his breath to ice inside his lungs.

He turned back to Cait. "Would you do me a favor, love? Put that ring back on your finger where it belongs, and then give your father the other package."

She studied him again from beneath long, dark lashes, then she bent and retrieved the ring she'd taken off fifteen months before, the diamond still smaller than she deserved but surrounded by even smaller diamonds in a way that managed to give the appearance of something larger. She brushed it with her fingertip and, smiling, handed it to him gently. His heart swelled and quickened as he slid it back on her finger and brought it to his lips. They stood a long moment only looking at each other. He would never tire of looking at her.

"You two going to stand there all day?" Donald asked from the couch, his voice gruff, though whether with impatience or some gentler emotion, Brice couldn't tell. "Or are you going to give me that package?"

Cait laughed, and Brice mentally shook himself, feeling warm with relief and joy. Cait walked the small, flat package over to her father, and Donald tore it open in a single quick motion as far removed from his daughter's careful approach as it was possible to get. But he stared at the painted salt dough frame and the photograph that Brice had glued inside it with his brow furrowed. "What's this, then?"

Cait moved over beside him. After standing very still a long while, she raised her beautiful eyes back to Brice, and her voice was very soft as she asked, "Whose bairn is this?"

He wanted to memorize every tiny detail of the way she looked as he waited for her reaction. "I found software online that let me upload photographs of the two of us to see what our child would look like. He's not exactly like I saw him in the loch, but he's as close as I could come."

She closed her eyes, then opened them slowly, and fixing on him again, she mouthed a "thank you" before turning to her father. "You said you didn't have anything left to live for, but a bairn needs a grandfather, and you're the only candidate. A boy needs to know where he comes from as he grows up. He needs to know all the things you taught Robbie. You were afraid you hadn't given either him or Mum the kind of life that they deserved, but if you look on that tree, you'll see a hundred smiles that prove you wrong. But whatever you think you missed, Brice and I are going to have the chance to get it right. Don't you think you'd better stay around and help us?"

Donald had dropped down onto the sofa as if his legs had given out beneath him. His gaze had been locked on the photograph in the salt dough frame, but now he turned to Brice and asked, "You saw Cait's son in the loch?"

"Aye," Brice answered. "Our son."

Donald was quiet for a long moment, and when he looked up his eyes were moist. "Well, we can't have him thinking he's all MacLaren. Maybe I'd better make certain I'm here to teach him a few things he'll need to know."

SPRING

*"From the ashes a fire shall be woken,
A light from the shadows shall spring;
Renewed shall be blade that was broken,
The crownless again shall be king."*

J.R.R. TOLKIEN
THE FELLOWSHIP OF THE RING

THE WAIL OF BAGPIPES AND THE BEAT OF DRUMS never failed to give Cait goosebumps when the notes carried across a starlit sky. On Tom-nan-aigeal, the knoll behind the present church and the ruins of the older kirk, the bonfire rippled like liquid gold, sending crimson plumes of smoke into the darkness. Shadowed shapes bundled in coats and blankets crossed in front of the light as people greeted each other, speaking in hushed, excited voices. In front of Cait, her father and Brice both labored up the path, her father with his cane and Brice with his single crutch.

Both of them were too stubborn to have her drive them.

Reaching the crest of the knoll, they paused, still wary of each other but united in their determination. Brando and Angus were the first to spot them and wave them over, and soon everyone was turning and calling a welcome: Flora Macara and Duncan in his Clan MacGregor kilt, who were passing mulled wine and hot cider around; Brando's Emma at the table with Davy Grigg's wife Lissa, serving steak pies, fairy cakes, and bannocks. Shame, the Macara's golden retriever, begged underfoot and did his best to steal any scrap of food that came within his reach. There were kilted pipers and drummers playing in both MacLaren and MacGregor plaids, and near them Mairi MacFarlane, who had worked at the Library and Tea Room, waved at Cait with a hopeful smile. Cait would need to speak to her soon and get her to come back, her and Kirsty Greer, as well, in some capacity or another. Kirsty herself sat in a chair with her legs stretched out and her hands resting lightly on her enormous belly, chatting with Iain Camm MacGregor's wife near the spot where Elspeth Murray stood with Jenny Lawrence, Mrs. Ewing, and the older women who quietly ran the Village Hall— and the rest of the glen, for that matter. All of them waved or smiled or called a greeting as Cait, her father, and Brice came up, but off to the side, Rhona Grewer and her twin daughters, Sorcha and Fenella, stood whispering unpleasantly with Brice's second cousin Erica as they saw Cait arrive.

They didn't matter, Cait decided. They were part of the fabric of the glen, the same as anyone else, and they had exactly as much power to upset her as she allowed them to have.

People trickled over, careful of Donald but eager to tell Brice how sorry they were about his accident. Many of them had taken the time to stop by the hospital, and others had brought food or cakes to the house—along with still more photographs of heroic women in their families—these past few days. Cait slipped her arm through Brice's and let him lean on her instead of on his crutch, the way they had leaned on each other in turns through most of their lives.

They'd both had missteps. Wavered. But that was the point of first love—trial and error, and learning to navigate the hardest and best and most important relationships of your life.

Most of the time, first love was outgrown and left in the past, or broken beyond repair. Cait and Brice had managed to come through it, and she had no doubt at all that they could come through anything life threw at them. Glancing up, she took in Brice's profile, the slight bump of the nose he had broken long ago, the hard, stubborn jaw, the faint tilt of lips that had been made for laughter and kisses and arguments that led to still more kisses and still more laughter. She intended to see he'd have plenty of all of those. He deserved every good thing she could give him.

As if he'd read her thoughts, he turned and looked down at her, then bent and kissed the top of her head. "All right?" he asked.

"Brilliant," she said, "and I still love you."

"Still?" He grinned at her.

"Always. Forever."

He kissed her again. "Good. And that still won't be long enough."

The pipers stopped, and the drums beat slowly, calling everyone back to the fire. Duncan looked to Connal MacGregor, who tried to shake his head. Duncan wasn't having any of that. "It used to be your grandparents who said the words of the Forgiving every year at Hogmanay," Duncan insisted, "and the rest of us think it's high time you stopped shirking your responsibilities."

Connal looked around, his tousled blond hair turned the color of flame and ashes in the firelight. He drew Anna and his daughter Moira closer beside him and cast his eye across the gathered crowd.

"The old year's been long and hard, but it has brought us many gifts," he said, which if they weren't exactly the words his grandparents had used, were close enough. "We look ahead with hope to what the new year will bring, and we use this opportunity to let go of the things that do not serve us well, to grudges that set us against our neighbors, to habits and hurts that make our footsteps heavier. Each one of us has baggage to burn, so let's begin."

A cheer went up, and he dug in his pocket as the pipers behind him launched into the first notes of "MacGregor's Salute." Connal took out a rolled-up slip of paper from his pocket and walked to the edge of the fire to cast it deep into the flames. A burst of glowing ash rose skyward on the hot rising air, then drifted slowly down again.

"Was that a grudge or a promise?" Brando called.

"A bit of both," Connal shouted back, laughing. "And I'll thank you not to ask."

Anna and Moira went next, and then others around the fire, the process accompanied by questions and good-natured teasing. That was the point of the Forgiving, when peace was restored and the small resentments of village life could be set aside.

Then it was Cait's father's turn.

Donald Fletcher hobbled closer to the flames, but what he pulled from the pocket of his old blue parka wasn't a single roll of paper. There were many. He tossed the first into the fire and pulled out a second, and then a third, a fourth, a fifth, a sixth, and a seventh.

The crowd started laughing. "You about done, now?" Duncan Macara asked him. "The flames'll go out at the rate you're going!"

Donald let his eyes sweep over the faces around him. "I've a lot to ask forgiveness for, and a lot to leave behind."

There was a brief silence at that, and since the pipes had long since stopped, the crackle of the flames and the rustle of coats and the call of a distant night bird suddenly seemed too loud until Elspeth looked hard at Donald from where she still stood beside Jenny Lawrence.

"And what are you hoping the new year will bring you, Donald Fletcher?" she asked.

He took a breath and turned to Cait. "Long life," he said, his eyes holding hers, "long life and the courage to face it."

He shifted again, smiling wryly, and his gaze swept around the circle, taking in all the faces of his friends and neighbors. "My Cait's getting married, in case anyone hasn't heard, and she's writing a history of the glen, and re-opening the Library and Tea room, and while she does all of that, all I'll have to do is *haud* my *wheest* and learn to walk again. Doesn't seem too hard in comparison, does it?"

A hoot of laughter went up, and Cait threw her

own old grudges into the fire. She took the hand her father held out to her and grinned up at him, thinking how the flame shadows and a bit of feeding had made him suddenly loom large again, thinking how coming through a hard winter together made every new day so much the brighter.

"The day you keep your opinions to yourself," she said to her father, "is the day my own tongue will be made of sugar, old man. But I wouldn't have you any other way."

Author's Note

ALTHOUGH I HOPE VERY MUCH this book feels real to you, it is a work of fiction, and the setting is a fictional place based on a real one that I enjoyed visiting. The Balquhidder Glen in the Scottish Highlands captured my imagination from the moment I stumbled across the inconspicuous little road sign for Rob Roy MacGregor's grave while driving down the A84. The time that I spent in the glen was magical, and it is truly one of the most beautiful places I've ever been. Because I didn't wish to do it a disservice, and because I needed to rearrange a few things to suit the story I was writing, I gave it a fictional counterpart in *Lake of Destiny*. Balquhidder is pronounced Balwhither, and so that's what I named the place where *Lake of Destiny* and *Magic of Winter* take place.

Officially, this is the third installment of the Celtic Legends collection. The stories are standalone, each complete in itself, but some of the characters are recurring and their lives continue. You'll find references to them as you read. For this reason, I do recommend starting with the first book, or going back to it to see where everything began. But you won't lose anything by reading out of order.

And now, for a brief note about the Christmas and Hogmanay, which is the last day of the year in Scotland. I mention in the book that Christmas was not officially celebrated there until 1958. Once Catholic, Scotland became Protestant after the death of James V in 1542 and the "rough wooing" of Mary Queen of Scots, who was eventually executed in 1567. That time saw what is called the Scottish Reformation, in which the country broke with away from the influence of the Roman Catholic church and developed a strong national and strongly Presbyterian "kirk," or church. Holidays like Christmas that were seen as predominantly Roman Catholic in influence were banned in 1560, as were older practices such as bonfires and particular types of song and dancing. Some of these reformations were taking place in other parts of Britain as well under the influence of Oliver Cromwell, but while the celebration of Christmas returned in England, it was not brought back as a public holiday in Scotland until the mid 20th century. In contrast, Hogmanay, whose roots may go back as far as the celebration of the winter solstice, took on greater significance and became a major celebration with a host of its own traditions.

Balwhither Glen, of course, loves nothing more than a celebration, and its traditions are its own. In keeping with the winter solstice idea behind Hogmanay, I've revived the practice of burning old grudges in *Magic of Winter*. And while the book takes place in December around Christmas and Hogmanay, its themes of family, loss, hope, redemption, and renewal are a perfect reminder that good things may be just around the corner at any time of year.

SPECIAL OFFER!

If you've enjoyed *Magic of Winter*, *Bell of Eternity* or *Lake of Destiny*, the next new destination in the Celtic Legends collection, *Echo of Glory*, will take us to Ireland, and *Heart of Legend* will take us to Wales. Look for them beginning in Spring of 2018 and order early for exclusive introductory pricing!

To stay on top of all the news, special offers, giveaways, and romantic recipes, sign up for my newsletter via my website (http://www.MartinaBoone.com) and stay connected.

ADULT FICTION AVAILABLE NOW

THE CELTIC LEGENDS COLLECTION
from Mayfair Publishing

YOUNG ADULT FICTION
AVAILABLE NOW

YOUNG ADULT SOUTHERN GOTHIC ROMANCE
from Simon & Schuster/Simon Pulse

Acknowledgments

Once again, without my wonderful and supportive family, this book would never have happened. Deepest gratitude as always to Susan Sipal and Erin Cashman for their brilliant editorial insight, generosity, and friendship.

Thank you as well to my lovely readers and friends, and to the booksellers and librarians who have been so supportive, and especially to my Advance Reader Team—to all those who have championed this series and my books. I'm so grateful to each and every one of you!

Finally, many thanks to Jennifer Harris and Amanda VanDeWege for their editorial wizardry, Kalen O'Donnell for yet another gorgeous cover, Rachel and Joel Greene for their beautiful interior design, and everyone involved at Mayfair who made all this possible.

ABOUT MARTINA BOONE

Martina Boone is the award-winning author of the romantic southern gothic Heirs of Watson Island series for young adults, including *Compulsion*, *Persuasion*, and *Illusion* from Simon & Schuster, Simon Pulse, and heartwarming contemporary romances for adult readers beginning with *Lake of Destiny*. She's also the founder of AdventuresInYAPublishing.com, a three-time Writer's Digest 101 Best Websites for Writers site and is on the board of the Literary Council of Northern Virginia.

She lives with her husband, children, a Shetland Sheepdog, and a lopsided cat, and she enjoys writing romances set in the kinds of magical places she loves to visit. When she isn't writing, she's addicted to travel, horses, skiing, chocolate flavored tea, and anything with Nutella on it.

http://www.martinaboone.com/